Love at First House

Love at First House

A COWBOY MOUNTAIN MAN / CURVY GIRL ROMANCE

ROUGH & READY COUNTRY
BOOK EIGHT

ENGRID EAVES

Contents

Chapter One

My eyes scan the Silver Fork, taking in the dark wood floors, black-painted booths with dark green upholstery, and brick walls. The earthy, smoky odor of freshly brewed coffee hits my nostrils as I spy Broderick with his salt-and-pepper shaggy hair and beard at a booth by the window. I head in that direction with a nod of my head.

He stands, and I reach for his hand, gripping it firmly and leveling my gaze on his steel-gray eyes. "Morning, boss"

"Morning, son, good to see you."

Broderick Montgomery owns the custom home design firm I worked my way up through after graduating high school and a few college semesters. Now that retirement looms, he wants to pass the baton, and I'd like to merge our two companies into one larger corporation that will dominate the West Coast luxury home business.

When I initially threw out the idea, he sounded hesitant, but I've never been one to take "no" for an answer. Today's meeting is about hashing out the details. At least if I have my way.

Vinyl squeaks as we each take a side of the booth.

Broderick removes the thick-framed black Raybans perched atop his head, placing them on the mahogany table top. I plop my tan cowboy hat next to them.

I ask, "How are the wife and kids?"

"Doing great," he pauses, laughing, "You know, my youngest continues to be a total fuck up. His mom spoiled him too much. I always warned her about that. But Maverick's made it through boot camp, and Cap is in his second year of law school."

"Good stuff. You've tanned up since the last time I saw you. How's that golf game coming along?"

"Breaking ninety these days."

"Nice. Well, I'm glad to see semi-retirement's treating you well. You have nothing to worry about from the business side of things with me on deck."

He nods firmly, but the ambivalence in his eyes doesn't escape me. Today's all about getting him over any lingering doubts that he has.

I feel a female presence hovering to my left and push my mug closer to the table's edge to make the server's job easier. The glug glug glug of pouring coffee greets my ears as I stare at Broderick's white chipped mug, which is still sitting on the side of the table furthest from our waitress.

He sighs, shifting uncomfortably in his booth. "That's what I wanted to talk to you about—"

A cheerful voice interrupts, "Coffee?"

Broderick looks up, annoyed. He gives an impatient nod. Before his eyes return to mine, however, he does a double-take.

I grab a creamer packet and open it as thick waves of scarlet hair graze the top of our table next to the creamer bowl. *That can't be hygienic.*

My last logical thought vanishes as my eyes trace their way

up the glossy tresses until they land on the last person I want to see. *Dammit!*

Her face is symmetrical and round, with plump cheeks and almond-shaped eyes. Thick black lashes frame emerald green eyes, shining with a depth and intensity that make my breath catch. Rows of lovely white teeth like pearls greet me, but it's the luscious thick lips I can't take my eyes off. She has a crease in the middle of her lower lip that I ache to run my thumb over before capturing her mouth with mine.

Her ivory skin invites me to touch her, all soft, supple warmth, the perfect complement to my rough, work-hardened hands. And her cheeks instantly darken two shades as our eyes meet. I loudly swallow the thick lump in my throat.

"Hi, neighbor," I manage, but my voice cracks at the end, a sound I haven't heard since my torturous pubescent middle school years.

Lily Monroe.

Fuck, she does this to me every time, and it makes me feel like a creep. I don't know her exact age, but she's way too young for me. Hasn't even finished college yet...

When her parents, Vera and Donovan, died tragically three months ago, the local newspaper said she left art school in Paris to return home to care for her five younger siblings. The first time I saw her was at their funeral, an ivory-skinned angel shrouded in black. The image stole my breath and remains seared in my memory.

Despite the age difference, I feel a strange pull towards her. As if fate wants to tie us together... I don't know why. Honestly, I run from understanding why because I refuse to take advantage of her. Maybe part of the connection is the fact I also parented my siblings from an early age. Hell, I even parented my mom... It was a disaster waiting to happen.

"Hi," she replies, pulling me from my thoughts. Her eyes

3

graze appreciatively over my face, making me feel like we're the only two people in the world. I wish we were.

I have so many things I need to say to this woman. For starters, keep your dog and his shit off my property, along with your mischievous little brother who keeps stealing my welding gloves and tools. But these very practical thoughts evaporate in the heat of her smoking curves.

Fuck! What in the hell are you doing, Turner? You're a thirty-four-year-old custom home builder on the verge of clenching your dream enterprise. You don't have time for college girls.

Broderick grabs her wrist, and my vision goes red. He may be the man who taught me everything, but my fists clench beneath the table, ready to knock the motherfucker unconscious. I grit my teeth together, opening my mouth to command him to let her go.

But before I can get the words out, he says, "Nice tattoos." My eyes go to the delicate pink peonies interwoven with a dainty black-and-gray snake, swirling down her lower forearm onto the back of her hand. It's sexy as fuck...

"Oh, these?" She chuckles, artfully twisting her wrist to evade his grasp. "Glad you like them."

I can tell by how she fluidly escapes him that she gets this kind of behavior often from men. My brows furrow, and I suddenly feel moody as shit. *Motherfucker.*

"Do you have more?" Broderick asks, ogling her.

Cutting in, I say, "Excuse the old guy for drooling. He may need you to bring him another napkin."

She shrugs and laughs, her eyes fluttering nervously to mine before looking down. "Do you boys know what you want yet?"

What I want? Is she really asking me this?

I stare at her like a dumbass idiot. *What do I want?* My

mouth hangs open, and all I can think about are her generous tits, luscious hips, and round ass. I want to run my hand through her silky hair and see if her mouth tastes as sweet as she smells. I want to wrap my arms around her and shelter her from the world. Of course, I want to make her scream my name, but even more than that, I want to make her love me. And that's the reason I have to avoid her at all costs...

"Napkins for this guy, too," Broderick chimes in, glaring at me across the table. "And give us a few more minutes with the menu, okay?"

Her cheeks remain as red as the tresses framing her face and snaking their way down to her waist. Even from this distance, I can smell the fragrance in her hair, like fresh, juicy strawberries. My eyes can't help but slide back down to those gorgeous thick thighs and curvy hips.

Thankfully, she walks back towards the kitchen, holding the steamy coffee pot she served us from. What my redheaded neighbor does to me is next-level. And now I can't even visit my favorite restaurant without having her assault my eyes.

It takes every ounce of willpower not to follow her with my eyes, but I stop myself, willing them back on Broderick's face. His bushy brows are raised, and he looks amused.

"My next wife has tattoos like that," he teases, and I feel my face burning, even though he always jokes this way. *What the fuck is wrong with me?* "Nah, I'm just kidding. She's way too young for me. Besides, my old lady would kill me before she let me divorce her. And the way that woman reads and watches true crime, she'd never get caught. It's the secret behind our enduring marriage."

Broderick's statement couldn't be further from the truth. I've seen very few men more devoted to their wives. But he's also a perennial jokester, which means nothing is off-limits.

"Speaking of old ladies, I'd feel much better about leaving

you the business if you settled down and married. You know, behind every great businessman is a greater woman."

The words hit me like a gut punch to the stomach, and I suck in air at the exact moment the coffee mug reaches my lips. So the drinking I mean to do turns into choking. Only it's not a one-and-done cough. It's a down-the-wrong-windpipe deal that leaves me spluttering and gasping for air.

"You okay, Turner?"

My throat tightens, and I raise my hand, palm up, gesturing for a pause.

Diners in nearby booths crane their necks to watch me, and the waitress I'm used to having, Roxanne, rushes to my side, patting my back and asking, "Turner, are you okay?"

I feel red in the face as I take another sip of coffee, nodding my head. I want to say, "I'm fine." But I can't get the words out.

The concern on Broderick's face gives way to amusement as I manage a couple of swallows, and my eyes quit bugging out of my head. Roxanne returns to serving other customers, and diners dive back into their meals. I'm relieved to be done with hogging everyone's attention.

Broderick remarks, "See what I mean? I can't even bring up marriage and settling down without you nearly choking to death. But Perfect Frame Homes is all about the image of family. We do more than build luxury houses. We create homes. That's a tough sell for a single guy so worried about commitment he nearly keels over at the mere mention of it."

I shake my head. "Coffee just went down the wrong pipe."

"Uh-huh." He side-eyes me, chuckling under his breath.

Roxanne stands over us now, her black braids whipping as she asks, "Do either of you need a warm-up?" Conflicted feelings grip me as I settle into the comfort of a familiar server while my eyes scan the room for that delectable strawberry.

How I can simultaneously thirst to see her, with every cell

in my body, while going to excruciating lengths to avoid her is...well, crazy. *But she's too damn young for me. Bottom line!* Coupled with anger and frustration over Broderick's judgment of my personal life, I wish this damn breakfast was over. Like yesterday.

Chapter Two

Roxanne stands at the counter in the kitchen, loading her tray with plates. She wears her long raven-colored hair plaited, and her crisp white button-down shirt contrasts beautifully with her bronzed Native American skin. She's got a full, curvy figure and a sunshine smile plastered on her face.

Coming up behind her, I whisper, "Roxy, I need a favor from you."

"What kind of favor?"

I hate asking others for help. But when I started working here a couple of weeks ago, she told me not to hesitate if I needed anything. And right now, I seriously, one hundred percent, desperately need a bailout.

"Is there any way we could switch a table?"

"Switch a table?" Her inky eyebrows shoot up into her hairline, and her warm, earth-toned eyes dance incredulously. "Why in the world would we do that?"

I bite my lower lip, choosing my words carefully. "There are these two guys at table three that I can't serve."

"Can't serve? Why not?"

I exhale sharply. "It's a really long story. But please. Could you do me this one favor?"

She leaves her loaded tray on the counter, heading to the kitchen door to peek through the small square window near the top. "Table three..." she says out loud before her eyes settle on the sturdy, rugged brown-haired cowboy with his soulful cerulean blues.

"Turner West?" The surprise in her voice mirrors the look on her face. "Hell, yeah, I'll take his table. Not only is he hotter than hell, but he tips well. Are you sure you want to give me his table?"

"I've never been more sure of anything."

She side-eyes me suspiciously, questioning, "May I ask why you don't want to serve him?"

There are many reasons I hate being a redhead—the inability to tan, freckles, people accusing me of having no soul. But at the top of the list is a complete inability to hide my feelings. I didn't know my cheeks could burn hotter, but now they blaze.

I open my mouth, but nothing comes out. How can I explain this to her when I can't even explain it to myself?

All I know is the sight of Turner makes my heart beat out of my chest. My cheeks flush, a tight knot seizes my throat, and a needy throb claims the juncture at the top of my legs. And when my eyes meet his, all of that physicality intensifies, sending neediness humming to the tips of my fingers and toes. It's almost impossible to serve a table under those circumstances.

Only one thing can satisfy feelings like these. But the last thing I'm interested in is getting tied down in the Sierra backcountry when my heart remains more than five thousand miles away in France. Besides, the cowboy makes it abundantly clear with the way his face scrunches, and his voice goes hard every time he sees me, that he can't stand me.

"Wait, isn't he your neighbor?" She scowls, knitting her brows.

I nod.

She opens her mouth, but Jerry, the imposing, linebacker-sized cook with a New York accent, yells, "What the fuck are you two talking about? The food's getting cold. Get back to work."

"Yes, sir," I respond.

Roxanne says, "Sorry, Jere."

I mouth "thank you" to her as she bustles past me to the door leading into the dining room, turning around to push it open with her back. She calls, "No, thank you." The flirtatious edge to her voice makes me second-guess myself as jealousy hits me like icy shards in a hailstorm. Suddenly, she pauses. "Where are you at in the service?"

"The first round of coffee."

"Alright, you weirdo, but you owe me." She winks, and an ominous feeling settles in my gut. Hopefully, part of that owing won't involve an explanation later. Besides, by the sheer delight on her face, it seems more like she owes me. The thought of watching her flirt with him... Ugh!

You begged Roxanne to take your table. Make up your mind, Lily!

My muscles relax even as disappointment creeps in, knowing I've shut down further interaction with my handsome neighbor. How can I feel so many contrary things at the same time? It's bewildering.

She pokes her head back in. "You get table eight. Mrs. McCreary just walked in."

Great. Mrs. McCreary is the one woman in Hollister bent on making a server's life miserable. It figures. As my brief twenty-one years on planet Earth have taught me, Karma's a bitch, and irony's her orgasm.

Ten minutes later, I stand over table eight as Mrs.

McCreary glares into my soul. "The coffee's cold and weaker than usual, and you gave me a dirty fork."

She holds up the silver utensil, pointing to an imaginary spot I can't see, even when I squint and draw closer. Everyone from Jerry to Roxanne and the afternoon server, Stacey, has warned me never to argue with this woman. But those are dangerous words for a redheaded Scorpio. I lead with anger far more than I care to admit.

So, I take multiple deep breaths, trying to smile widely. *You have to do this to keep your family together. Think of the bigger picture.* I comply with her every wish and demand until I've done about three times the work at her table as anywhere else in the dining room. She still leaves a measly two-dollar tip.

Whenever I head to the kitchen, my eyes wander to table three. The gorgeous cowboy does an excellent job of immersing his gaze in the wall when I pass. It confirms what I already know. He hates me.

Roxanne spends far more time chatting and flirting with Turner's table than any other in the restaurant. It makes me simmer, although I'll never admit it out loud. Even though she's doing me a huge favor, I'd like to slap the smile off her face.

A part of me also smarts at how relaxed and laid-back the tall, dark-haired cowboy looks with her as opposed to me. None of that weird, tense eyeballing and prickly body language. I'm not sure what I did to earn his bad side. But I thank God for it because I don't know what I'd do if he felt the same for me as I do for him.

That's a total lie.

I know exactly what I'd do...

The tight pulse at the top of my jeans doubles down, and I let out a resigned sigh. I guess he will always make me feel this way. But considering the state of my parents' affairs and my inability to earn even half of what my dad made as a home inspector, I doubt we'll be neighbors for much longer.

Roxanne brushes past me in the kitchen, blowing a stray lock of black hair out of her face. "What did you do to Turner?" she asks under her breath, trying to look busy for Jerry while she whispers to me.

My heart jumps at his name. "What do you mean?"

"He was coughing up a storm when I got to his table. I thought I would have to do the Heimlich maneuver or something."

"I didn't do anything other than serve him and his friend coffee."

She shrugs, saying, "I call dibs on him. From now on, if he comes in, I get his table." I chew the inside of my cheek at the lusty look on her face.

"Does that mean you're trading me for Hawk?" I tease, clearing my throat. He's a good-looking Native American helicopter pilot who comes in often with Sheriff Christian and Logan, the search and rescue guy. They're all foster brothers, according to small-town talk, and I know Turner fits into the mix somewhere, too. But I'm still trying to figure out this town and its people.

"Hell, no," she counters, her cheeks darkening. Thank God I'm not the only one who blushes around here.

Chapter Three

TURNER

On-site custom home inspections take me from the outskirts of Truckee to North Lake Tahoe and Stateline. In Truckee, I meet the homeowners for the fifth time to discuss countertops and backsplashes in the kitchen and bathrooms. The house is a behemoth at more than five thousand square feet with a massive eight-car garage that makes me drool.

In North Lake Tahoe, I hash out permits and scheduling for our next project. And in Stateline, I have it out with a new subcontractor.

"West Homes comes with an implied standard of excellence. We leave nothing to spare when it comes to the details and materials used. But this is shit. Pure shit, and it has to go," I demand, pointing at the poorly laid tiles in the entryway. "A grade-schooler could do a better job."

Todd scowls, looking down. "Can't find a tiler worth his shit these days. It's a pain in my ass."

I nod. "Now, it's going to be a pain in your bottom line. I want this shit done yesterday and don't make me have another conversation like this with you. Plenty of other subcontractors around here are chomping at the bit to complete a West Home. You hear me?"

Todd glares, nodding his head in defeat.

They say custom homebuilders are like orchestra conductors. Trying to get an ensemble of individual musicians to play as one. To me, it feels more like being a head chef, contending with an endless stream of mediocre cooks, burned food, and grease fires.

On my way home, I stop by the Hollister gas station to fill my tank. A handwritten note, torn from a spiral-bound notebook, reads: "Temporarily out of order. Please see attendant."

If I had a dollar for every time this happened, I'd be a billionaire rather than a millionaire. But what do you expect from a gas station run by the town drunk? Functioning drunk, that is.

Striding towards the convenience store, I finish up a call with the homeowners from the Stateline property. "Yep, I never like delivering this kind of news, but I wanted to keep you apprised of the situation. I appreciate your patience and understanding. Have a good evening."

I shut off my phone as I walk inside towards the unmanned counter. Thanks to the mediocre quality of my new subcontractor's work, I had to push the project finish line back a couple of weeks. It's a conversation I never like having.

I ring the bell impatiently. *Where the fuck is Craig?*

"Coming!" A female voice calls from behind me, and I glance over my shoulder towards the back of the store. The delectable profile of a woman with waist-long scarlet tresses steals my breath, and my eyes hungrily devour her from head to toe, lingering at her curvy middle as she restocks the six packs of beer. Fast on the heels of appreciation follows fierce anger. *Seriously?*

She looks over her shoulder, and my eyes lock with hers.

Stopping dead in her tracks, she stands immovable, her cheeks darkening like red wine bleeding into a white tablecloth.

I grumble the first thing that comes to mind. "You work here, too? Since when?"

Her eyes round, and she shrugs her shoulders. "Pretty much since I've been back in town."

"No way," I reply testily. "I'm in and out of this gas station all the time. I would've seen you."

Her brows furrow, and I see something resembling anger snatch control of her eyes. "I usually work the night shift when I'm not serving at Stonie's."

My mind spins at her answer. "Do you mean to tell me you have three jobs?"

She looks down, avoiding my eyes. "Yes." She hurries behind the counter, asking, "How do you want to pay?"

I hand her my company credit card, careful to avoid touching her hand. But my mind's still going a million miles a minute. Before I can filter my words, I spurt out, "I don't want you working the night shift here. Your dad wouldn't like that."

She looks up, and her sparkling greens hold my gaze. The air sizzles and crackles between us. I swallow so loudly that I know she can hear it.

"There's a lot that my dad wouldn't like that's happened lately," she says, defiantly lifting her chin. "But I'm out of options—"

"And working at Stonie's? I never knew your mama especially well, but I can't imagine she'd be okay with that. Are you even old enough to legally serve alcohol?"

She sets my credit card down on the table, laughing bitterly. "No offense, mister, but how is this any of your business?"

"It isn't." I shake my head. "But somebody has to say something."

Putting her hands on her hips, she cocks her head to the side. "Not only am I old enough to serve alcohol, but I'm old enough to have lived in France, learned the language, and attended art school. And, I might add, I am old enough to raise five children all by myself. Would I like to do things differently? Of course, but it's not like fate asked before taking my parents."

Her voice cracks on the last words, and remorse floods me. But I can't let go of this. It may not be any of my business, but the last thing I want to see is this pretty little thing's face plastered on the Missing Persons board at Walmart.

I growl, "Life's shitty. I get it. Which is even more reason why you don't put yourself in dangerous situations that could get you harmed or killed." *You're too beautiful for a place like this.* I bite my tongue hard to hold back the last words.

"And what do you know about shitty lives?" She challenges, her eyes narrowing.

I laugh. "More than I care to remember. I was a foster kid."

"And that's exactly what I'm trying to keep my sisters and brothers from becoming, which requires making ends meet, no matter what it takes."

"Surely you can find better jobs than this."

"You try finding a decent-paying job in this podunk town. Especially with an unfinished art degree."

"I don't need to find a job, Strawberry. I made one for myself."

"Strawberry?"

My face reddens. *Did I really just call her that? Shit.*

"And may I ask why you're calling me 'Strawberry?'"

My face warms. "No reason. It just suits you."

"Well, while we're on the subject of nicknames, asshole suits you."

Her words strangle an unexpected laugh from me, and my

cock jumps. There's something incredibly sexy about her fiery stubbornness and sharp tongue. All the more reason she needs to stay safe. "Yeah, I am. But that's not what this conversation's about. No more night shifts at the gas station or Stonie's. You hear me?"

Bitterness tinges her words as she replies, "I don't know what you think gives you the right to talk to me like this. But I'm done with your bullshit, and I'm done with your opinions. Every time I see you, you make it abundantly clear how much you despise me, although I have no idea what I did to deserve it. It makes the fact you think I care about your opinion even richer."

Her words sting, and I don't know why. But I push the curious feeling aside. Instead, I rack my brain for a different angle, one to make her consider my message. "So, who stays with your brothers and sisters when you work here and at Stonie's? Aren't they a little young to go unsupervised? Especially at night?"

She raises her chin defiantly, "My sister Poppy is twelve years old and fully capable of watching everyone. I was babysitting neighbor kids just as young."

I shrug. "But four younger siblings? Hell, that'd be a handful for an adult."

Her expression fractures as my words find their mark. I don't enjoy doing this to her, but the woman needs to listen to reason. Her eyes swim as she looks down, and it takes every ounce of my willpower not to round the counter and pull her into my arms. *Why the hell am I nursing such a sweet spot for this bratty, barely legal woman?*

Looking up, her eyes plead with me as she says, "I'm doing the best I can. When is it going to be enough for this shitty ass town and shitty ass hicks like you? I thought you people were all about keeping families together, not pulling them apart."

Hicks? You people? There's so much here I don't know

where to start. Instead, I focus on her jaw-dropping, verdant eyes, noticing how she tries to discreetly wipe tears from them with the back of her hand.

"Look, I didn't mean to make you cry. But you've got to start taking better care of yourself. Quite frankly, you're too young to be strapped down with a mess of kids—siblings or not. Besides, there are worse things than being in foster care. I turned out okay. Maybe you just need to let them go."

Her face glows with rage as she runs my card and aggressively hands it back to me. "Turned out okay is debatable. But then I don't remember ever asking for your opinion, asshole. Have a nice day!"

Lily storms from behind the counter towards the stocking area, and I holler, "I mean it about those graveyard shifts, Strawberry. You need to be home at night with your doors locked."

She slams the door to the back, and I let out a frustrated snarl. Nobody ever talks to me this way, and it's a total fucking turn-on. I wish that's all it was, though. The tangle of emotions accompanying every interaction with my neighbor makes my head spin and my heart ache.

Need infuses every one of these emotions. Need to protect and cherish her. Need to make her life easier and shield her from the world. Need to be there for her, no matter how abundantly clear she makes her disinterest for me. Truth be told, I need to leave her alone, but I can't make myself do that.

Does that make me a masochist or something? Most gals fawn on me because I'm not bad on the eyes, and I'm rolling in money. But motherfucker, if this disagreeable and mouthy woman didn't just give me a hard-on. More reason to keep my distance...

Chapter Four

LILY

Craig stumbles through the gas station door at ten past eleven, which I've grown accustomed to with him. The smell of whiskey follows him, which doesn't surprise me, either. Small towns talk, even to new arrivals, which means I've heard my fair share of shit about his status as the town's "functioning alcoholic." Watching him weave towards me, I'm not sure functioning is the right word, though.

"Lily, doll, how are you?" he asks, melodramatically dancing towards me.

I don't know what it is about the folks in this town, but they all have a nickname for me. 'Doll' is by far the most common endearment. Although I have to say "Strawberry" still has me shaking my head.

Frustration hits me as I reflect on my earlier altercation with Turner West. I'll never understand why God created such a handsome specimen of manhood only to make him a total asshole. The good Lord must appreciate walking irony the way Karma does.

"I'm fine, saucy. You look pretty happy yourself."

"Saucy?" he straightens, blinking and staring at me.

I smile sheepishly. The nickname-giving doesn't appear to go both ways.

"Thanks again for switching shifts with me." I've been trying to move my shifts to swing instead of graveyard so that I can pick up extra hours at Stonie's when the crowd justifies it. That said, I've already received a text from Stonie saying that tonight is out. My throbbing feet welcome the news because I've been standing all day, but I could use the money.

"No problem. It won't always work with my schedule, but we'll play it by ear on a week-to-week basis. Do you have any plans for tonight?"

I laugh. The idea of having plans outside of work seems ridiculous, even though it would have been the norm four months ago in Paris.

"Well, I'm ready for a hot bubble bath, lighted candles, and music. If Poppy's done her job, the kids should already be in bed."

He nods. "Did you have any trouble today?"

I shrug. "An asshole cowboy, but nothing I couldn't handle."

"Glad you've got the asshole cowboys figured out. We get our fair share of them around here."

I chuckle, still unable to fathom why Dad and Mom wanted to move here from San Diego two years ago. If they hadn't relocated, maybe they never would have been killed in the car accident. And perhaps I never would have had to abandon my art school ambitions and life in Paris to rush home for my siblings.

Thinking about it in this way makes me sound so selfish, though. My parents lost their lives, and we lost our parents. A pretty city and higher education don't trump any of that. Instead of fixating on the past, I need to focus on the future and how to keep my family together, no matter what short-term sacrifices it requires.

"You look sad, Lily. What's wrong?"

Big, fat teardrops well in my eyes despite the deep breaths I take to calm myself. I bite my lower lip, shaking my head.

"It's got to be tough taking care of so many kids. Do you really need to work three jobs to make ends meet?"

I look up, unceremoniously wiping my eyes and nose on the sleeve of my thermal. Yeah, it's gross, but there isn't a tissue in sight. "If you saw the pile of bills my parents left behind, you wouldn't ask me that. Not only were they at the beginning of a massive mortgage, but they took out private loans to facilitate their ambitious homesteading plans."

Selling the cabin will get us out of most of this debt. However, the local realtor advised me not to put the property on the market until spring. Until then, I must bide my time, keeping the title free and clear.

He rounds the counter, side-hugging me, accompanied by powerful whiffs of whiskey. I keep my body rigid, making my boundaries clear. Craig is in his late fifties with a stringy gray-and-black mullet. But you can never be too careful, especially when someone's under the influence.

Letting go of me, he shrugs, "Enjoy the rest of your night, doll, and I'll see you back here tomorrow. Same time, same place."

"Yep, thanks, boss." I start towards the back, biting my lower lip. The other thing I've learned about small towns is that people do a lot of talking to the wrong people. While everyone snickers behind this man's back about his drinking problem, no one will address it to his face.

My mother's words fill my head. *If you don't have anything nice to say, don't say anything at all.* I don't know if her advice fits the current context, though. The thought of Mama puts a lump in my throat.

I used to take for granted calling and talking to her. I did it every day. This is just the type of situation in which I'd pick her brain for advice. She was a wise and insightful woman who was excellent at putting things in perspective, even if I didn't always appreciate her truth-speaking and tough love. Apart from a couple of voicemails, I'll never hear her speak again.

On the way to the house, I stop at the mailbox, finding a thick clump of bills that make me instantly nauseous. I fantasize about burning the envelopes but dutifully tuck them in my purse. I'll go through them tomorrow, adding up owed sums until I cry. It's become my new norm.

I struggle to unlock the front door without a porch light. I always tell Poppy to leave it on, but she more often than not forgets. One of these nights, a bear or mountain lion will surprise me out here. We've captured enough of them on the wildlife cam out back, along with deer, coyotes, bobcats, foxes, badgers, and raccoons.

Inside, I step over piles of toys and blankets, sighing in defeat. I've always wanted to be a mother. Talk about the ultimate creative act. And the thought of bringing a precious little life into the world, nurturing them, and watching them grow warms my heart. But becoming an insta-mom of five bratty younger siblings who refuse to obey and contribute is another matter entirely.

Heat flashes in my cheeks as I flip on the light, scanning the room. The four-letter word "mess" doesn't do it justice. Cole must've gotten a hold of another can of silly string because pink and blue strands color the carpet.

The laundry sits in a chaotic pile on the couch even though I left it out earlier in a hamper with a clear directive to Poppy to fold it. I know Mama expected as much from me, as well as ironing, when I was a teenager. But my parents spoiled my younger siblings, babying them in a way they never did me... Maybe it's because they went so many years without more kids, assuming I was it. Or it might have had something to do with the second wind they got in their marriage after Dad retired from trucking and traveling all the time.

Either way, my dad's constant presence meant a quick succession of much younger "surprise" siblings. So did the desire to move to a rural location and start homesteading. I still don't understand why they chose Hollister. I'm nine older than Poppy. Essentially, we had very different parents in different places in their lives.

A cushion ramp indicates an afternoon sledding session in the hamper down the pillows. At least they didn't use the stairs this time. The last thing I need are ER bills on top of everything else.

Plates of half-eaten food sit on the coffee table. *Wait, why hasn't Trix licked them clean? Where is Trix?* My ears catch whimpering and faint scratching on the kitchen slider.

Those kids are going to get him killed if they keep forgetting to bring him in before they go to bed. As a Weimaraner, not only is his coat too thin for extended stays outside in the Sierra Nevada Mountains, but he's no match for a mountain lion or bear.

I pile the plates of food together and hurry into the kitchen, adding to the precariously high stack of dirty dishes. Then, I rush to the sliding glass door to let the dog in. He jumps on me, licking my face, and I order, "Off." The verbal command doesn't work until I gently nudge him in the chest with my knee to get him down.

Have the kids fed the chickens and gotten eggs? I doubt it. I'm not a massive fan of doing it late at night because bobcats prowl after dark...along with mountain lions and bears. But I have no choice.

Chapter Five

LILY

Heading back into the kitchen, I tear apart the messy counter before locating my headlamp and grabbing the big metal bucket I keep by the sink for retrieving eggs. Despite just letting him in, I call for Trix to follow me outside. I need him to act as my alert for any large animals on the prowl.

I should carry a gun or pepper spray with me when I do this at night. After all, bobcats are nothing to mess with. But my feet ache, I'm exhausted from a full day's work, and quite frankly, I only have so many steps left in me.

Outside, the familiar strains of "Free Bird" by Lynyrd Skynyrd reach my ears, and I see the lights from the asshole's massive workshop glowing. The music is quiet enough not to be heard in our house. But I hope his presence will provide an additional big predator deterrent. There has to be at least one pro of having the grumpy cowboy as my neighbor.

Dad built the big A-frame run and coop, and Mom stained the wood red so that it looks like cedar to match the cabin. It marked one of the many homesteader projects they undertook after getting inspired by YouTube to become self-sufficient and move to hick land. I have to hand it to them. They did a fantastic job making it sturdy and impenetrable. It looms ominously in the dark as I shine my headlight around the perimeter, ensuring no animals wait for me.

Despite the music in the distance, the hen house remains as quiet as a tomb. But as familiar motions sound my arrival, a few faint coos greet me. Sure enough, eight eggs are still in the house, and the girls act like they haven't had scratch today. Their feed bucket's nearly empty, and their water's low.

Dammit! Is there nothing I don't have to do myself?

The neighbor shuts off his music, and I wonder if he's calling it a night. Why should I care? Turner West stands for everything I gladly fled when I moved to France—an obnoxious redneck without one ounce of sophistication. I've often wondered what he works on in his workshop. But I highly doubt it's anything of interest to me.

I put my focus back on the chickens. Despite the lack of a rooster, two hens insist on going broody, day in and day out. I guess nobody ever explained the birds and the bees to them.

They sit on unfertilized eggs, dedicated to impossibility. The white one acts relatively gentle, usually moving out of the way when I reach under her. But the black-and-white speckled one gets cranky and pecks at my fingers.

Compared to a rooster, her bites barely sting. But I imagine her beak pinches provide enough deterrent to scare my sisters and brothers from their collecting duties.

I pick her up now, finding a clutch of beautiful multi-hued eggs beneath her. I collect them, marveling at the spookiness of the headlamp reflected in the eyes of the chickens and the knowledge just about any animal could be sneaking up behind—

"Glad to see you took my advice about Stonie's," a male voice rumbles over the fence.

The sound catches me so off guard that I drop the two

eggs I'm transferring to the bucket, letting out a strangled cry. The eggs make a hollow cracking sound on the ground. *There goes tomorrow's breakfast.*

I clutch my hand to my chest, breathing hard as I hear deep, dark laughter float in my direction. At my feet, Trix crunches away, already making quick work of gobbling the two smashed eggs.

Turner West.

Again.

Do I really have to see this top-notch asshole everywhere?

With my hand on my hip, I turn, eyeballing my neighbor's head over the fence. He looks away quickly as the light from my headlamp assaults his eyes. "Ahh," he grumbles. "Turn that thing off."

I return the favor of him laughing at me by chuckling at his reaction to the unwanted light. *Petty, I know. But whatever.* After a wicked moment's hesitation, I click off the headlamp, ready for another round of bickering with the archaic cowboy mountain man.

"If you must know, Stonie didn't need me tonight."

The light from Turner's shop backlights his face as he scowls at me. "You seem drawn to danger, girl. What's your deal?"

"First of all, I'm a woman, not a girl. Second, what do you mean 'drawn to danger?'"

"Chicken eggs aren't worth a possible altercation with a—"

"You can save your breath. I know what's out here. But considering I started work at six this morning and just finished, it's my only option."

"You sure do a lot of talking about all the options you don't have."

I can't argue with that statement. Instead, I nod. My breath catches in my throat as I notice how the moon's pale light glimmers across his face's angular planes. His jaw is square and rugged, and his cheeks darkened by afternoon stubble. I wonder what they would feel like beneath my palms...

Stop it, Lily!

But it's too late. The tension at the top of my legs returns. It's hardly the reception Rough & Ready Country's chief jerk deserves. His gorgeous blue eyes linger over my expression, and my cheeks glow.

Suddenly, he clears his throat, saying gruffly, "I've been meaning to tell you something."

My heart jumps. "Yes?" My voice shakes with rogue anticipation. It's like my body is in full mutiny around him...

"Keep your dumbass dog and little brother off my property. You hear me?"

He couldn't blindside me more if he slapped me in the face.

"I've got dog shit all over my backyard, and somebody keeps stealing gloves and tools out of my workshop. If you don't get this under control, I'm calling Animal Control and the appropriate authorities."

I inhale sharply, gripping my fists at my sides.

"Trespassing and stealing are crimes. I don't care if your little brother's a minor—"

"He's nine years old and just lost his parents," I manage before the gruff cowboy cuts me off.

"Trespassing is trespassing, and stealing is stealing. Period. Consider that my first and last warning." His eyes narrow over the last phrase, and his jaw tightens until a muscle bulges.

Under any other circumstances, the look would be sexier than hell. But I'm too busy fantasizing about pelting him with eggs to appreciate it. I'm sure he'd press charges for an egging, too.

He runs a hand through his thick brown hair, usually

27

buried beneath a tan cowboy hat, and nods goodbye. The false show of politeness makes me steam.

"Thanks for letting me know how you really feel, asshole."

"That's all you'll ever get with me..."

I shake my head, standing my ground and waiting for it.

"...Strawberry."

I let out a frustrated growl. Damn, I hate this guy. Out of all the people in Gold County, why does he have to be my neighbor? Now, I regret switching tables with Roxanne. I should've used the opportunity to spit in his coffee.

A gorgeous and unexpected smile lights up his face. It makes my pulse pound and my panties dampen, even as I fantasize about slugging him. Yet, while my thoughts burn, he turns and walks away like he couldn't care less. I hate this man. I'm so angry that my body shakes as I fume, thinking of a thousand snarky retorts after the fact.

Chapter Six

TURNER

"For fuck's sake!" I scream, shaking my fist in the air. I swore that if another pair of my gloves turned up missing, there would be hell to pay. And I'm a man of my word. But the knot in my stomach holds me back. There goes my Friday mini-vacation and attempt to get ahead on my next commission.

I pick up my phone, ready to call the authorities. *Who the fuck else could it possibly be?*

Doubt holds me back, though. *What if I'm wrong?*

The face of a burgundy-headed nine-year-old boy flashes in my mind. Cole Monroe. Less than an hour ago, I caught him sneaking around my property...as usual. When I confronted him, he used retrieving his dog as an excuse. But the kid's a little shit, compounded by the near-constant lack of supervision. That fresh piece of news is something I only discovered last night, thanks to his mouthy, gorgeous older sister.

I shake my head, trying to clear the stunning woman's image from my mind. She's not beautiful in any classical sense of the term. More like otherworldly, even arresting. And unfortunately, it's the exact kind of arresting that makes my blood heat.

Talk about irony. Never have I longed to get my hands on a woman more. Or do everything I can to make her and her brood of brats move. As for Cole, one thing remains true, whether I call the authorities or relent. The little fucker needs to learn a lesson about taking other people's shit.

I pull off my welding helmet and set it unceremoniously on the work table before grabbing my cowboy hat and sauntering to the fence separating our properties. A few paces in, I breathe hard as the anticipation of seeing—and no doubt fighting—with Lily floods me. Arguing seems to be the only thing we're good at, although the pace of my heart and over-sensitive cock make it clear there are plenty of other activities I'd like to try with her.

Dammit.

I hop the back fence. Yeah, it's trespassing. But under the circumstances, I feel justified.

Trix, the family's silver Weimaraner, is instantly on me barking. The muscular hunting dog probably weighs about sixty pounds. Everything except for his black nose is the same gray color, giving him the appearance of a streamlined, four-legged ghost.

His tail wags, and he jumps up on me, licking my neck. "Down!" I command brusquely. That's another thing that's changed since the death of the Monroes.

Trix is constantly on the loose, wandering through my backyard and leaving behind stinky brown presents. A quick scan of the fence line shows me where he's dug underneath. No wonder.

I give him a quick scratch behind the ears before repeating, "Down!" This time, the smoke-colored canine obeys. Wiping the drool from my neck, I stride towards the front of the house. Why I'm doing this instead of calling the proper authorities, I don't know.

Didn't I tell her last night's threat was my first and last?

That said, I've had time to think about things. I can't get my foster dad's voice out of my head or his words. *Everyone deserves a second chance.*

A mid-February chill bites my flesh, demanding a coat. But I'm still hot from a morning spent welding and even hotter knowing that bratty-ass kid stole one of my welding gloves.

Everything about the backyard screams kids. Toys lie scattered everywhere, and a treehouse positioned low in a thicket of evergreens begs for repairs and a paint job.

Donovan, the father of this crew, would have been on top of it. The guy worked as a home inspector and loved woodworking. Some of his handmade furniture even found its way into the custom luxury homes that I build. Although we were never close, seeing how things have fallen apart without him is sobering.

I follow the path around the side of the house to the front door and bang on it loudly, circumventing the doorbell. Screams and scrambling echo inside, and I thank my lucky stars that I'm single. Donovan and his wife, Vera, left six kids behind after the accident. *What a fucking nightmare!*

Clicking and thumping indicate someone struggling with the lock. Then, the large, dark green door slowly opens, and Poppy sticks her head out. She's got strawberry blonde hair, turquoise eyes, and the rough-and-tumble appearance of a tomboy. She wears her softball uniform from last year, the Rough & Ready Bobcats, and her hair hangs in messy braids.

"Yes?" She asks, staring up at me hesitantly.

"I need to speak to Lily. Is she around?"

The reddish blonde shifts her weight from one foot to the other, and I can tell a thousand thoughts wrestle in her mind.

"Why are you asking?"

I don't know if she's got a hearing problem, but I hate repeating myself. Gruffly, I reply, "I need to speak to Lily."

A strong whiff of smoke hits my nostrils, and I look over her shoulder into the mayhem of four unwatched, redheaded children. The house is a mess, something I never would have seen while Vera and Donovan lived, and the burning odor intensifies by the second.

Poppy pulls back, about to close the door on me. But the smoke smell requires investigating.

Cole, the little shit I'm after for lifting my gloves, tears into the entryway, screaming what's obvious, "Fire!"

And Poppy's face twists.

The fire alarm screeches, and I push through the door as Poppy moves back, resigned to my presence. Following the thick cloud of smoke billowing towards me, I chase it into the kitchen, where the stovetop looks like a bonfire.

"Where's your fire extinguisher?" I ask, turning to find a row of scarlet-headed kids in every shade from wine to copper lined up in descending order by height, with the twins, Jack and Rosie, leveling off at the end. Ten rounded eyes in shades of blue and green stare expectantly at me. No one says a thing.

Flames engulf the stove, sending thick, inky columns of smoke into the air. Fire licks up the wall towards the microwave, threatening the cabinets above the stovetop.

"Where's your fire extinguisher?" I repeat more loudly, striding towards the pantry and opening it. I scan the small space, finding bare shelves and an overflowing trash can.

Wheeling back around, I demand, "Baking soda. Where's your—"

Before I can finish speaking. Cole runs forward with a glass of water, launching a liquid stream at the flames.

Lunging forward, I snatch him backward as the fire explodes into a molten column of sputtering sparks and white-hot flames that lick the walls and ceiling.

Hasn't anybody taught these kids about fire safety?

Smoke burns my lungs and eyes, darkening the air. Inhaling it can't be great for kids.

"Where's Lily?"

"At work," Daisy replies, her voice cracking. Having lived by the Monroe's for two years, I know Daisy's younger than Poppy by a touch. In my opinion, neither girl is old enough to manage their mischievous younger siblings. But as Lily and I established yesterday, my opinion doesn't matter.

"Is there anybody else here besides you five?"

Daisy shakes her head, making the auburn curls on her head shake with the effort. Horror crystallizes in her aqua eyes as she stares past me at the kitchen inferno. Crackling flames reflect in her wide, blank gaze.

"Everybody outside," I order, hustling the kids towards the front door. I pull my cell phone out of my back pocket and dial 911. Outside, Trix circles the kids, barking and wagging his tail.

The dispatcher answers, and I give him the address of the house fire. He pauses. "The Monroe place? Hasn't that family been through enough?"

I rub my hand over my face and watch black smoke pour from the cabin. "Hell yeah, they have. But life isn't fair and never has been."

"You've got that right."

I answer countless questions until the distant sound of an engine catches my ears. "The firefighters are almost here."

"Are you okay with me getting off the line now?" asks the dispatcher.

"Yes, thank you."

For thirty minutes, I watch Hollister's volunteer fire crew

tackle the flames and smoke seeping from the house. I wonder how many of these guys my brother, Travis, knows. He's a wildland firefighter, so he wouldn't typically take a call like this. But I recognize his supervisor, Kurt, who works off-season in town.

As the men and one woman bustle to get the blaze under control, I get a call on my cell phone from my brother, Christian. He's the sheriff of Gold County.

"Hey, bro."

"I heard you called in a fire at the Monroe place. Are you there now?"

"Yes."

"And all of the kids are accounted for?"

"Yes, they are," I reply.

"Just wanted to let you know Conner's on the way. So, if you could hang out long enough to make a report, that'd be great."

"Sure thing. I'm not going anywhere until someone shows up who can care for these kids, anyway."

"I've got that covered, too."

"Is Lily on her way?" I ask, feeling the telltale thud behind my ribcage that always accompanies me speaking her name.

"No, but Darlene at Child Protective Services is."

"Fuck," I say before catching myself. Fortunately, the kids are too engrossed in watching the firefighters to pay attention to me cursing.

My brother knows how I feel about CPS. Out of all of my foster brothers, I'm the one who experienced the most trauma at their hands during removal and separation from my mom and siblings. Hell, the memories haunted my nightmares for years. Even now, a cold sweat breaks out on my forehead.

"Yeah, I know," he replies. "That's why I wanted to warn you. This situation's been coming to a head for a while now, Turner. There's nothing you can do about it."

Christian may be my older brother by a hair, but I hate it when anyone says that shit to me. *There's nothing you can do about it.* I've never been one to take "no" for an answer or limit my options. It's what makes me a top-of-the-line home-builder. But just this once, I admit my brother may be right.

Chapter Seven

LILY

Ten minutes into my fifteen-minute break from the Silver Fork, I whisper in French into the phone, fighting sobs as I pace up and down Main Street. Passersby give me quizzical looks. Some open their mouths like they want to inquire if I'm okay. Others look off-put by the foreign language I speak.

I've avoided this call for far too long—letting my advisor at art school know I won't return.

"This is terrible news, Lily."

"I know," I mutter, wiping the hot tears drenching my cheeks with the back of my hand and sniffling.

"You do know how prestigious your scholarship is. Don't count on getting a second chance at it."

I reiterate that I'm sure about withdrawing from school and giving up the rest of my scholarship. *Why does it feel like I'm ripping out my soul?*

The call ends, and I return to the gravel lot behind the dumpy diner. The Silver Fork may look quaint and cute from the front, but this area could use some work. It doesn't matter,

36

though, because the only people who ever see it are vendors delivering orders.

Staring at weeds starting to push through patches of pavement, I fight hard not to scream and throw my cell phone. In one fell swoop, I surrendered my education and future career in the heart of a dynamic city for a small-town hell hole. It was the right thing to do, the only thing I could do. But that doesn't make accepting my new life any easier.

Jerry comes wheeling out back, the giant's eyes wide and his face contorted. "Lily, where have you been? I've been looking all over for you."

"What is it?" I ask, knitting my eyebrows together. The strange look on his face robs me of all embarrassment despite the tears still drenching my face. Besides, he's used to seeing me cry. It's my favorite pastime since relocating to Hollister.

"It just came over the scanner." His words don't surprise me. Jerry listens faithfully to local police, EMS, search and rescue, and firefighter transmissions. And I can kind of see why. Nothing else of interest goes on in Rough & Ready Country unless you like horses and cows. "Firefighters are heading to your house."

"What?" Fear seizes me.

"I heard it plain as day. Fire at the Monroe house."

I cover my mouth with my hand, shaking my head. *How much more can I possibly take?* My legs feel like they could buckle under me, but the adrenaline's flowing too fast to allow it.

"I've got to get home."

He nods as I race past him, grabbing my purse and keys.

"Keep me posted on what's happening," he calls after me as I blaze past Roxanne without any explanation and race out to my car. I still wear my apron, and my hands shake as I unlock my car door.

On the way, I dial the elementary school to ensure my

siblings are okay. To my horror, the school counselor confirms they missed the bus again this morning. And Poppy never made it to the middle school. *Dammit!*

Fifteen minutes later, I tear down the long gravel driveway to the cabin, seeing thick black smoke rising in a column ahead. I've never been much of a praying person. But now, I open the lines of communication to heaven, fervently pleading for divine intervention. Turner's ominous warning fills my head. I should have never left the children unattended. But what choice did I have?

A big red fire truck sits in front of the house, and fire-fighters douse the cabin's roof, fighting angry, smoking flames. My eyes flash from the yellow-clad men to the five redheads standing in the driveway, their mouths gaping. I count them twice to ensure everyone's accounted for. To my relief, so is Trix, exuberantly lunging towards the firefighters.

A big, burly man holds him back. The same drop-dead gorgeous cowboy I try to convince myself I never want to see again. He's squatting, and my eyes linger over his ass-hugging jeans and white thermal as they showcase every inch of his rugged, angular planes.

Turner looks over his shoulder in my direction. My eyes dart to his face, caught mid-ass stare while my cabin burns. *What in the hell is wrong with me?*

I rush over to him. "What happened?"

"What's it look like? Your siblings set the kitchen on fire, which probably wouldn't have been a big deal. Except I couldn't find your fire extinguisher to save my life."

Instead of answers, his response stokes a firestorm of questions. Chief among them: What is he doing here?

He lets go of Trix, and the gray puppy lunges into my arms. I grab his collar, searching vainly for a leash.

"Put him in your car with the windows cracked," Turner commands. The authority in his voice annoys me.

But I comply, in no mood to fight. I return to stand beside him, and my sisters and brothers crowd me.

Poppy says, "It wasn't my fault. I was just trying to make pancakes, and—" She bursts into tears, and I pull her into my arms, comforting her as I survey the scene.

Turner looks warily over his shoulder at me. "There was a grease fire on the stove. And then Cole here—" He ruffles my brother's hair as if he's known him for ages. "Decided to throw water on it. Do you know what happens when you pour water on a grease fire?"

I nod. "You *are* talking to a waitress at a diner..."

He frowns, his soulful sky-colored eyes penetrating me. "They're too young to be left unattended—"

I cut in. "Poppy is twelve years old—"

He glares at me.

"I don't know what else to do. I'm—"

"Let me guess. You're out of options." His voice crackles with bitterness.

Rosie and Jack, the six-year-old twins, each take a leg, hugging me tightly. "It was so scary," Rosie whispers in her tiny, smoky voice.

Jack nods his head emphatically.

The cowboy adds, "Lily, like it or not, you need help."

I shake my head, fighting back a new onslaught of tears as my eyes shift to the firefighters. They no longer hose the house, which I read as a sign of progress. "Yeah, I know I need help. But nobody's offering."

"Child Protective Services is en route."

"Why?" I ask breathlessly, panic snatching my heart.

He side-eyes me. "You may not see it now. But this is for the best."

I turn towards him, rage flaring. "How is breaking up a family for the best?"

He scowls, replying, "When my bio mom could no longer

take care of me and my siblings, going into foster care was... necessary." There's an edge to his voice that tells me there's a lot more to the story. Turner averts his eyes, suddenly reluctant to make eye contact with me. His voice trails off. "You might not see that now, but—"

"You and I both know that's a load of bullshit. And we're not talking about you. We're talking about me and my family. I'm fully capable of taking care of my siblings if somebody would just give me a damn break."

He shrugs. "In that case, you'll explain things to CPS, and everything will be fine, right?" But the grim look in his eyes says otherwise.

In the distance, I see two cars wending toward the house. A sheriff's deputy car and an unmarked black SUV that has visited before. I'm no stranger to CPS, especially with my guardianship pending. But seeing that car here, under these circumstances, fills me with a dread so visceral I can taste it.

Gut-wrenching desperation floods me, and I turn to my neighbor, begging, "You say I need help. Well, help me, then. Please. I'll do anything."

The look on his face is unreadable as the muscles feather in his jaw, and his brows furrow. His eyes narrow, dissecting me, and I feel naked in front of him.

Why I appeal to this asshole's sense of decency, I don't know. But despair overrides all reason and pride. I'll do anything, literally anything, to keep my family together. So, I say again, my eyes large and moist, "Please help me, Turner. I'm begging you."

Chapter Eight

TURNER

The woman standing in front of me is a walking contradiction. The hate pouring off her in my direction is undeniable, even though I caught her ogling my ass a few minutes earlier.

She's the paragon of responsibility, working her fingers to the bone to pay the bills and keep her family together even as she fails to recognize that no good can come from leaving four kids ten and under home alone with a preteen.

Something in her pleading eyes reminds me of the person I've spent my whole life trying to forget—my mother. Not because I don't love and miss her but because thoughts of her come with unbearable anguish no amount of time can soften.

Too young to be a mama, too artsy to function in the real world, and too addicted to bad men and drugs for a decent life. In other words, a walking disaster.

CPS had to take us away. There was no other way. But the ancient ache of getting ripped from my mother's arms and separated from my brother and sister still smacks into me hard.

Visceral. Palpable. A cold sweat breaks out on my forehead, and I rub my temples, feeling dizzy and nauseous.

Even worse is the obvious realization that one snap of my fingers could make all of Lily's pain disappear. Funny how money can do that.

I swallow hard, steeling my gaze at her as Officer Conner Murphy and a CPS worker head our way, accompanied by my brother Travis's supervisor, Kurt.

Thankfully, I've known Conner most of my life, although I'd rather have my brother, Christian, here. And as for Kurt, I could call in a favor from Travis. But the CPS lady is a newcomer to Rough & Ready Country and a wild card.

"Are you the owner of this house?" Kurt asks the fiery beauty, and she nods, stunned into silence. I much prefer her spitting defiant insults. But now she looks terrified.

One snap of my fingers. That's all it would take... And it could help me clinch the deal with Perfect Frame Homes, to boot...

Motherfucker.

A clammy dread crawls over me as the CPS worker introduces herself as Darlene Wilkins, shaking my hand and then Lily's. I can tell by the look on the older woman's face that there's only one way this will go.

I should leave before it gets ugly. "Miss Monroe, were you here when the fire started?"

Lily shakes her head hesitantly. "No, I was at work."

Darlene says, "I see." Her voice contains the same icy edge I remember hearing from officials the last time I saw my mother and siblings. "And why weren't the kids in school today?"

The redhead looks at them, her eyes narrowing. But her siblings look away, refusing to make eye contact with her.

This is not my fucking problem, and I don't need to put myself through any more of this. Still, I can't suppress the disorientation that grips me.

CPS has to do this, Turner. There's no other way. After all,

Lily's siblings nearly burned their cabin to the ground. It could have started a wildfire that ravaged my property and countless others in the neighborhood.

It could have resulted in the deaths of one or more of the scarlet-haired kids huddled together. But as five pairs of large eyes drill into me, another sickening wave of memory-induced emotions slams into me.

This is not your problem, Turner.

But the reality remains undeniable.

Entertaining one stray thought brings a quick succession of others. Maybe I was put here for a reason... After all, this is all too fucking ironic to be anything but fate. Right?

Conner's eyes catch mine, and he nods to the side, gesturing me to follow him. I pace behind the clean-cut, brown-haired deputy in his tan-and-black uniform, feeling my stomach swim as thought gives way to persuasion. It doesn't make the plan forming in my head any less idiotic, though.

"What exactly happened here?" he asks.

"Well, I came over to the house to...check on the kids. And I noticed the smell of smoke coming from the place."

"Check on the kids?" he eyes me curiously. "Is that something you do often? Especially when they're supposed to be in school?"

"That was a mistake," I say flatly.

Looking back at the family talking to Darlene and Kurt, I know deception's the only way out. But I still don't want anything to do with it. Lily's expression contorts as she darts through too many emotions to read. Rosie and Jack cling to their older sister's legs, and Cole's gaze pans my way.

His eyes plead with me. I might as well be staring at myself as a kid. Even though he still needs to learn a lesson about not stealing, I can't help but know exactly how he feels as more painful echoes from the past grip me.

There's nothing worse than seeing a family ripped apart.

Except being a part of that family. With mine, it was necessary. *But is it really in this case?* I remember Lily's words about "needing a break."

Out of everyone in this town, I'm best equipped to give her one. But is it the right thing to do? Or would she take advantage of me for my money? With how hard the woman works, and how unwilling she is to accept help from anyone, I can't entertain the last question in good conscience.

"Well, I thought she was too young for me...at first."

Conner's gaze drills into me.

"And maybe she is. But she's legal." I shake my head at the last sentence. Dammit, I sound like a fucking creep. But then, I've never been especially good with words, and I'm even worse with lies. "I mean, this whole situation is legal. I just wish I'd come to my senses a lot sooner. We could have avoided today's scene altogether."

What the fuck am I saying? What the fuck am I thinking? I muddle through the words, registering the deputy's skeptical face.

Daisy lets out a cry. "No, I don't want to go!"

My eyes gravitate to the kids and Lily, and a knot grips my stomach. As I watch the Monroes, I relive the single most painful episode of my entire life. Only instead of being a helpless child with no ability to alter the outcome, I'm an adult millionaire with every resource at my fingertips.

That is, if I can deal with the consequences.

"Fuck it. Why can't I be more of an asshole?" I whisper under my breath.

"Come again," Conner asks, cocking his head to the side.

My voice sounds wooden as I force out a lie, "I've been an asshole. But enough's enough." This goes against everything I believe in, but for some reason, it also feels like the right thing to do. *How can that be possible?*

The image of Darlene attempting to pull Rosie from Lily's

leg cements my resolve. I stride towards Lily, wrapping an arm possessively around her and pulling her firmly against me. I don't look at the redhead's face because I can't stand the thought of the contempt my move will inspire. But I say a silent prayer that she'll get the gist and play along.

To Darlene, I say, "There's no need for that."

The salt-and-pepper-haired woman scrunches her face, and her head bobbles back and forth between Lily and me. "These children have no place to stay, thanks to the house fire. Furthermore, the state needs to reconsider their current custody arrangement."

Just play it cool, Lily. That's all you have to do.

I finally look down at the breathtaking woman, willing her to follow my lead. A flicker of recognition flames in her eyes, and she rests her palm on the juncture of my chest and stomach. Sparks flicker at her touch, although the adrenaline of the moment keeps them from flaming into something more.

"This is all my fault. I should've made it official sooner."

"Made what official sooner?" Darlene questions, eyeing us both.

I nearly choke on my words, turning towards Lily. "I think it's time to move up the wedding date... Don't you, Strawberry? And you and the kids are staying at my place from now on."

I've lost my fucking mind.

I steel myself, prepared for the venom that usually floods Lily's gaze at the sight of me. Instead, she glares resolutely at the older woman, nodding her head. Her eyes flutter to mine, flooded with confusion, relief, and gratitude.

"Wedding date?" Darlene sputters, shaking her head.

I say the first thing that comes to mind. "The rest of my brothers are getting hitched. I figured it was my turn."

Darlene's eyes shoot daggers at me, and she opens her mouth to speak.

But Lily cuts her off, smacking my chest harder than she needs to. "Baby, that's not the only reason you're marrying me."

"Of course not. But the other reasons are...well, private." My words are anything but convincing. But I've never been good at making up stories on the fly...

And as a bachelor, I have no clue what in the hell makes people get hitched anyway. Done with words, I go for action to persuade the small crowd gathered. Leaning down, I plant a kiss firmly on Lily's lips.

The warmth and taste of her mouth ignite a blaze inside me as incinerating as the one Cole started when he threw water on the kitchen stove. Pulling back, I exhale sharply, my head swimming with contradictory thoughts. My body throbs with a deep ache like none I've experienced before.

Shit and fuck. What the hell have I done?

Chapter Nine

A new intensity storms in Lily's verdant eyes, and I'd give every ounce of my worldly wealth to know what she's thinking.

"Why haven't I heard about this from your brother?" Conner inquires, referring to Christian. I've known Conner since grade school, which makes pulling the wool over his eyes all the more difficult.

"Is that a customary practice at the Sheriff's Department? Sitting around and shooting the shit about your personal lives on the taxpayer's dime? If so, this is news to me. I guess I can call my brother to learn more about the rumor swapping."

The deputy shakes his head quickly. "No need. Point taken."

Lily exhales loudly, looking up at me. Her huge doe eyes search my face for the reassurance I am uniquely positioned to give. Decision turns into determination. I can't stand idly by as her family gets fractured before my eyes. Fate put me here for a reason. I make an internal oath to do whatever it takes to keep her family together.

Darlene's eyes remain trained on me. "If you're getting married, where is Lily's engagement ring?"

I pause, racking my brain for an answer as a suspicious silence settles.

"I never wear it to work," Lily butts in. "I know you don't like hearing this, babe, but the tips are better when I don't have it on."

The outlandish statement knocks the wind out of Darlene. She opens her mouth to speak but says nothing.

Every inch of this narrative might be fake, but the thought of any fiancée of mine not wearing my ring to get better tips still irks me. This being a small town, I'm sure that'll be the next rumor to circle, too. Well, along with the perverseness of me marrying a near-teenager.

I grumble, annoyed, "That stops this instant, Strawberry. If you need better tips, you come to me. You hear?"

Lily's face goes red, and Darlene shakes her head.

Conner laughs stiffly. But I can tell by his expression he doesn't buy the story. Not one bit. In fact, I can see the internal struggle between skepticism and childhood loyalty written on his face.

"Look, I'm not here seeking anybody's approval. And yeah, Lily's too young for me and could do a whole lot better. But what's done is done. And considering the situation, I'm taking matters into my own hands. Sweetie, pack your bags. You and the kids are moving in with me this afternoon."

Turning to Darlene, I add, "We'll be married by the end of the week. If you have any questions, please direct them to my lawyers."

The CPS official licks her lips, glaring at me. "You can throw your money and influence around as much as you'd like, Mr. West. But it's not as simple as you claiming to be in a relationship with Ms. Monroe. I'm taking the children into custody."

Lily's face is panic-stricken as she looks up at me, and I step forward to stop Darlene from seizing the twins.

The woman raises her eyebrow, threatening, "Do you want to be charged with obstruction of justice?"

I'm sweating bullets as the conversation takes me back to a time I've spent my whole life trying to forget. Clearing my throat, I work hard to control my voice as I say, "You may take them, but don't waste your time looking for placements. My lawyer will be at the office by the time you return. So, why don't you save these children the trauma of separation and let them pack their bags and head over to my place?"

She seizes the twins' hands, leading them towards her SUV as they break into confused sobs, crying out for their sister. Calling over her shoulder towards Conner, Darlene orders, "Officer, please help me with the older children."

Lily lunges forward, but I stop her mid-stride, holding her tightly against me. I whisper, "Don't do anything to make this worse."

"But...but..." She breaks down crying, and I do the only thing I can, given the circumstances.

I pull her into my shoulder, stroking the long ruby-colored tresses flowing down her back and reassuring her, "We'll have them back tonight. I promise."

Her hair smells like fresh, juicy strawberries. But I can't think about that now. I have to focus on keeping Lily's family together.

Conner orders Poppy, Daisy, and Cole towards the SUV. The little thief looks over his shoulder at me, his face torn. Poppy puts her head down resigned, and Daisy tries to run back towards Lily, but Conner stops her.

"You wait right here," I order Lily, letting go of her and striding towards Darlene.

The kids scramble into the SUV, and she wheels around, staring a challenge at me.

"I'm serious about Lily and the kids staying with me. There's no need to take them—"

"Mr. West, if you are indeed marrying Lily Monroe, we can discuss other custody arrangements later. But as it stands, I'm not permitting them to move in with someone who appears to be little more than a stranger trying to intervene out of the kindness of his heart."

I swallow hard. "Are you calling me a liar, Darlene?"

She shrugs. "We can revisit custody arrangements after you provide me with proof of your marriage."

I look inside the vehicle, seeing five pairs of scared eyes pleading with me for help. I feel an arm wrap around my waist. Lily's at my side again. Every muscle in her body is tense, and I can feel her willpower sapping as she works hard not to run towards the SUV.

I more firmly pull her against me to ensure she wins the raging internal battle. Returning my gaze to Darlene, I command, "Like I said, don't bother working on placements. Not only will you be hearing from one or more of my lawyers this afternoon, but you'll have a marriage certificate on your desk by the end of the day."

Darlene raises her eyebrows and smiles patronizingly. Slamming the back door to the SUV, she says, "I look forward to speaking with your lawyer." Rounding the SUV, she hops in the driver's seat and unhesitatingly turns on the engine.

Kurt grabs my attention, saying, "I need to speak with Lily, please."

"And you and I could use another chat," Conner chimes in.

I shake my head. "All future communications should be directed to my lawyers."

Conner nods, but Kurt steps forward, saying, "I didn't say I wanted to talk to you, Turner. I need to speak with—"

"The same goes for my wife," I growl, letting my hand

slide across Lily's back and down her right arm until our fingers are entwined. Those two words, "my wife," feel strange on my tongue, and I have to work hard to say them fluidly in a sentence. "How's the structural damage, Kurt? Can Lily go inside to grab a few things?"

The firefighter nods, looking irked. "Fortunately, we contained it to one room, and there are no signs of structural damage. But I wouldn't recommend sleeping there tonight."

"Lily and the kids will stay with me from now on," I reply firmly.

My watch reads ten forty-five on Friday morning. If we don't hurry, Lily could go a whole weekend without the kids. And they'll have to experience the trauma of separation and placement in foster homes scattered throughout Rough & Ready Country and maybe well beyond. A cold shiver runs down my spine as I flashback to the terror of being taken from all I knew and loved. I was no older than Poppy at the time.

My stomach clenches at the thought of the needless trauma. "Come on, Strawberry. We've got a courthouse to get to."

Chapter Ten

The burly cowboy walks me up the front porch stairs of the cabin, letting go of my hand. "Find something pretty to wear. Preferably white. Meet me at my truck in fifteen minutes. I have to grab a couple of things from my cabin."

My eyes shoot towards the car where Trix sits in the driver's seat, looking through the window.

"What do we do with the dog?"

Turner suggests, "Can we leave him in the backyard or your garage?"

"He'll get too cold."

"Well, he can't be left alone in my house while we're gone."

"Not even in his crate?" I question.

"In his crate's fine, I guess," the mountain man replies begrudgingly. "Conner, you mind helping me with the dog and his crate? He doesn't bite."

The officer nods, stepping towards my car as Turner follows me into the house, still airing out from the fire. It smells like a box of burnt matches. I point towards the crate in the living room, and he strides towards it, grabbing it as if it weighs nothing, and beelining for the door. "Hurry up," he grumbles before heading outside.

I stand frozen by the door, watching through the screen as he walks toward Kurt, Trix, and Conner. He reiterates, "We have no further comment. You both know where to find me. Now, I'd appreciate you vacating our property as soon as Conner here is done helping me with this trouble-maker." His head tips down, looking at the dog.

I've never heard anyone talk to authority figures like this before, and it's hotter than hell. I've always had a thing for bad boys, but I never would have guessed Turner West had an inner rebel streak. He comes across as so conservative in public.

Fifteen minutes later, Trix is in his crate inside Turner's cabin, gnawing on a Greenie. I stand outside Turner's white GMC dually, wearing the only light-colored dress I could find. It was my mother's church outfit. It's a floral sundress in ivory with large, abstract flowers all over it. It fits a little tighter than I like, enhancing my curves and cleavage, and it shows more of my tattoos than I've ever displayed around this town. Due to the chilly February weather, I cover it with a long black trench coat, one of my favorite purchases while living in France.

Turner reappears, looking harried. He talks on his cell phone, barking orders to what I can only guess is an employee. Curiously, he holds a large glass vase, filled with a stunning arrangement of white lilies, peach roses, peach carnations, and sage-colored succulents. He impatiently hands it to me before opening the passenger door and motioning for me to get in.

Shutting the door behind me and jogging around to the driver's side, he jumps in, buckling his seatbelt and turning the key in the ignition. As we start driving, he grunts into the phone, "Look, I've got to make a few phone calls. But I'll be in touch before the hour's up. So, look for my call."

My stomach lurches as the conversation ends. I don't know where to start thanking my neighbor for his generous actions. And I fear the awkward conversation sure to follow about tying the knot with someone who makes it abundantly clear every time he sees me that he can't stand me.

Not ready for this subject, I ask breathlessly, "Where did the flowers come from?"

While he backs up the truck, he explains, "My maid always leaves a bouquet after cleaning my house. Finally came in handy." He stops and looks at me for a long, awkward moment. "Get on your cell phone and figure out how to apply online for a California marriage license and get an appointment at the courthouse. I've got to make some phone calls."

Turner's one-sided conversations accompany the thirty-minute drive to Ophir City. He speaks with various lawyers, including a man named Flynn, whom he calls "brother."

Unless there's more than one Flynn in this podunk town, Turner's talking to the gorgeous black cowboy lawyer who frequents the Silver Fork with his girlfriend and paralegal, Jasmine. Sometimes, I see Flynn having breakfast with his adopted dad, Wyatt, too.

Next comes a call to Sheriff Christian that I'd give anything to hear both sides of. Turner barks into the phone, "Before Conner gets back to you, bro, I just wanted to let you know Lily Monroe and I are getting hitched at the courthouse this afternoon—"

A long pause follows, and I can hear a male voice on the line, but I have trouble making out words apart from "crazy" and "waitress." He's another semi-regular at the Silver Fork, and I thought the good-looking, though gruff, blond Sheriff appreciated my fast service and attention to detail. After all, his tips are always generous. But damn if I don't feel discontent and bewilderment pouring through the phone now.

Clearing his throat, Turner growls, "First of all, I didn't

ask for your opinion. Second, it's none of your goddamn business. Third, if anyone asks...well, you say whatever you like. But you can no longer act surprised."

There's another long silence. At the end, the grumpy cowboy says, "Well, it's not like you keep me on speed dial when it comes to your love life, either. Hell, I knew for twenty fucking years that you were in love with Cricket. But I had to learn about you finally hooking up with her one week after the fact and second-hand from Zane. So, consider the favor returned. Now, quit talking down to me like a fucking older brother. I'm only a couple of years younger than you—"

A third long pause has me straining to hear what's going on. Finally, Turner's voice sounds begrudging as he finishes, "Yeah, what the fuck ever, bro. I love you, too. Bye."

"Sounds like that was some phone call..." I say, fishing for information.

"Thanks to the generosity of my adopted dad, I have fourteen pain-in-the-ass brothers. Two down, only twelve more calls like that to go. Well, eleven since I mostly communicate with Holden through emails and letters."

I raise an eyebrow.

Turner shrugs. "He's in prison for manslaughter."

"Oh my!" I exclaim before catching myself.

Side-eyeing me, he asks, "You having second thoughts about marrying into my family?"

I open my mouth, but no words come out.

"Good," he grumbles as his phone rings again, and he fields more work calls.

As I fill out the online form on my phone, I have to interrupt his conversations to ask for personal information. I learn that his full name is Turner William West. He's thirty-four years old and has never been married.

After I type in this information, he side-eyes me, clearing

his throat. "So, lay it on me. How old are you, Lily?" His face grimaces in anticipation of my answer.

"Twenty-one," I reply, defiantly lifting my chin.

"Fuck, I was afraid of that. This whole goddamn town is going to think I'm a pervert."

"Well, are you?" I ask.

"Hell no!"

"Then, why do you care what other people think?"

He growls, "Because you're thirteen years younger than me."

"I'm surprised it's only thirteen years."

He raises an eyebrow. "Explain, please."

"Well, you act like a boring old guy. So, I thought you were a lot older than thirty-four."

"A boring old guy? What's that supposed to mean?" he grumbles cantankerously.

"Case in point," I answer.

He growls low in his throat. I've never heard a sexier or more dangerous sound in my life.

Swallowing hard, I explain, "Well, for starters, it's obvious you're set in your ways, and you go around handing out advice like you're someone's grandpa. No offense...especially considering what you're doing for my siblings and me. But you asked."

"Yeah, I did. I'll make a mental note to only ask you questions when I'm prepared for the answer."

"Smart move," I quip. "My friends and family would tell you it's the easiest way to avoid getting hurt by me."

"Not possible," he cuts in assertively. "Only people I care about can hurt me."

"I can't argue with that," I reply. "Although it's tough to believe you don't care about me, or at least my family, considering what you're willing to do for us."

"Well, if Christian's right, I've lost my fucking mind. Is that enough reason for you?"

I press my lips tightly together. As much as I want to take the bait and keep quibbling with him, the last thing I need is my Good Samaritan rethinking our fake marriage. *What would I do then?*

I go back to a much safer topic. Asking questions for the marriage license application.

He lists his parents as Ruby Jean Moore and Wyatt Harrison. I've never heard of a Ruby Jean in Hollister, but I've spoken to the cute old cowboy named Wyatt before. I'm guessing he's in his seventies, yet he's far less grumpy than this son of his. Now, I get the connection between Turner, Flynn, Christian, Logan, and Hawk. They're all foster brothers.

Finally, I declare, "The marriage license is submitted. But there's no way we're going to get an appointment at the courthouse on such short notice." Up to this point, my actions have run on adrenaline and hope. But now my voice cracks, and I feel defeat creeping in.

He side-eyes me, his face somber. "There's always a way."

This launches a new round of phone calls to lawyers, including Flynn. Once everything sounds straightened out, he goes back to work phone calls.

By the time we park in front of the Ophir City Courthouse, he's put out countless work fires and solved too many problems to count. The man may be grumpy and crude on the phone, but his decisiveness, knowledge, and problem-solving skills can only be described as impressive.

Turner jumps out of his white dually, greeted by a man in a suit. He pats the man on the back, and they converse seriously for a few minutes before both men round the truck.

Turner opens the door and offers me his hand. As I get down, sparks of electricity jump between our flesh, and his eyes wander to mine. His nostrils flare, and his jaw tenses before he looks away.

"Lily, you need to sign these papers." The cowboy hands me a pen.

"What are these?"

"A prenup," he says matter-of-factly.

I shuffle through the papers quickly, incapable of concentrating on the legalese. At this point, I'd sign away my soul to get my younger siblings back. The thought of their terrified faces as Darlene took them flashes through my mind.

After I finish, Turner scratches his autograph next to mine.

"Did you have any luck with our appointment?" he asks the man in the suit.

"You should be up within the hour," the attorney replies.

The words shock me, and I ask, "How did you do that? There were no appointments left for today."

Before the lawyer can answer, Turner replies, "Money talks. And lots of money does lots of talking, especially in a small town like this."

Looking at the lawyer, he says, "I'll call when we're done and heading towards Social Services. In the meantime, get a hold of Darlene's supervisor, and don't let her place those kids. You hear me?"

"But do you have a witness?" the man asks, nodding towards the courthouse.

Turner nods. "There's a tiler on his way over who owes me one."

The cowboy starts to shut my door but stops when he sees the bouquet in the vase balanced on the passenger seat cushion. Pulling it out of the truck, he unceremoniously removes the flowers and dumps the water before putting it back in the truck and handing me the bouquet, their stems still dripping.

"Try not to get that on your dress," he orders in the same authoritarian voice he uses for his employees.

Normally, I'd retort with a snarky comment. But I'm so overwhelmed by everything that's going on that I feel like I'm staring at the scene from outside of my body. Everything about the last couple of hours feels surreal. Instead of talking, I hold the bouquet, trembling as we head into the courthouse.

Turner grabs my free hand, squeezing it tightly. Stopping, he looks over his shoulder, observing, "Lily, you're shaking. Are you okay?"

I nod firmly, but he doesn't look convinced. So, I add, "I'm just worried about my sisters and brothers."

His eyes narrow, and he gives me a confident nod. "Let me worry about that now, Strawberry. You ready for this?"

"I could ask you the same question."

Grimly, he replies, "You don't want to hear my answer."

Chapter Eleven

LILY

I stand in line at the Ophir City Courthouse, awaiting our turn in the Justice of the Peace's office. Sure, this place is the county seat. But I still can't wrap my head around why the place is packed.

Looking at my phone screen, I realize why. It's February fourteenth—Valentine's Day. I'm lucky to get a single rose or card on this day, let alone a whole hunky husband.

Turner paces back and forth a few feet away, frowning and taking more calls. I catch snippets of his conversation.

One of his subcontractors isn't pulling their weight, and he's pissed. The tongue-lashing he gives isn't for the faint of heart. Of course, I've had enough experience bickering with him that such rebukes no longer phase me. But the fact I stand in line waiting to marry him is another subject. That little tidbit remains beyond my ability to process.

"Lily Monroe and Turner West."

My heart jumps.

The cowboy looks up, saying into the cell phone. "I've got to go. My number's up." He ends the call, walking past me to a guy who walked in about fifteen minutes ago wearing a dirty

Carhartt jacket and torn workman's jeans. They shake hands, heading towards me.

Turner catches my eyes as he goes by, nodding towards the office. "Let's get this over with."

Inside the justice's office, I remove my trench coat, fold it, and place it on an empty chair. Turning around, I catch Turner admiring me. His eyes transform from cerulean to navy as they rove over me unabashedly.

His cheeks darken, and his nostrils flare as his gaze sweeps over the rose, lily, and bird tattoos on my décolletage and both upper arms.

I half expect him to run out of the room screaming, as he's never seen this ink before. Everything about him exudes repression and neuroticism. I can't imagine he likes tattoos.

To my surprise, however, he looks more like the big bad wolf ready to devour me. Letting out a loud exhale, he says quietly, "You're gorgeous, woman."

It's the first time he hasn't called me "girl," and it takes my breath away. I'd like to hear him say that more often. My heart beats erratically, and I swallow loudly. "Happy Valentine's Day."

"Shit, is it really Valentine's Day?" He chuckles.

The judge nods, concern flooding her face.

"No wonder the place is so busy," he grumbles. But his eyes wash over me tenderly, as if he enjoys looking at me. This is a new development compared to the past three months.

Our marriage may be fake. Turner's expression and reaction couldn't look more genuine, though. And I know the warm feelings they inspire in me are one hundred percent authentic. These emotions are worlds away from my feelings for the grump when we argued at the gas station and in the backyard.

Justice Mariah Powell motions for me to stand by Turner. She has brown hair streaked with white and beautiful cinnamon-hued eyes with a graveness that matches the somber mood. "Well, aren't you two the picture of love," she says, and I look down, trying to hide the heat in my cheeks.

Turner can't stop fidgeting as Judge Powell asks us to face each other. I clutch the bouquet with both hands until my knuckles turn white. Swallowing hard, I look away, reminding myself this is for my sisters and brothers.

My heart pounds out of my chest, and I barely make out the judge's words, staring down at the pastel flowers. A finger snags me under the chin, nudging my head upwards, and Turner nods, frowning grimly. His eyes scold me to keep my gaze on him.

I swallow loudly, my cheeks burning as my eyes settle on his. If he wants me staring at his face, I'll stare. But it doesn't mean I'll like it.

Only this last thought couldn't be further from the truth. Because, in reality, he's the most breathtaking thing I've seen in a long time. Rugged, masculine, authoritative, confident. The polar opposite of the immature losers and users I normally date.

The thought of Turner standing next to any of those guys puts a smirk on my face. He'd easily tower over them all, outstripping their girth by two times. *Is this why some girls dig older guys?* I always thought it had to do with a daddy complex, something I never had, thanks to my amazing father. But the uber-masculinity Turner exudes could make my ovaries explode.

The cowboy must misread the smile on my face, assuming it's for him because his face softens, and his eyes fill with a warmth I'm not accustomed to seeing. His lips turn up at the ends, and the reaction looks awfully authentic for a fake marriage.

It's also contagious. Against my will, my smirk transforms into an ear-to-ear smile, and my groom swallows hard, grabbing my right hand and slipping it away from the bouquet to hold. The move shocks me. Sparks from his touch tease the flesh of my fingers and palm, and my mind wanders.

Would I feel these same sparks in other parts of my body if he touched me there? The need is back at the top of my legs, more demanding than ever.

"Repeat after me. I, Lily Monroe, take you, Turner West, to be my lawfully wedded husband..."

My voice cracks as I repeat the words, straining to hear and repeat what the judge says.

"To have and to hold, from this day forward, for better for worse, for richer, for poorer, in sickness and in health, to love and cherish as long as you both shall live."

The blood pounds in my temples, making it hard to hear the judge's words, and I struggle, going quiet for a moment.

The scowl returns to Turner's face as I ask the judge to repeat herself. I'm having trouble with the "as long as we both shall live" portion of the vows because I've never been good at lying. Even when it counts. I take a deep breath, trying again. My voice cracks, but I muddle my way through to the end.

As the judge turns to Turner, his face twitches, and he rushes through the pledges. His expression looks hard, and his eyes narrow, gazing at me as his hand grips mine more tightly.

For a man whose voice normally booms through a room, his projection sounds surprisingly soft. His eyes go unreadable at the end as he clenches his jaw, making a muscle jump amid his handsome five-o'clock shadow.

"Would you like to exchange rings?" Justice Powell asks, and I shake my head.

But Turner says, "Hold on." Letting go of my hand, he digs into his jeans pocket, pulling out a small box. Staring into my eyes, he explains, "You deserve much better than this. But it belonged to my biological mother, and it holds a lot of sentimental value to me."

His voice is thick with emotion, and I don't know if he's telling me this to make sure I don't lose it or for another reason. Frustration grips me as I wish I could read the grumpy cowboy better. But he's got a poker face to rival any Texas Hold 'Em champ.

My head swims as I stare at the modest diamond on a gold band. "I'm sorry I don't have anything for you."

"We'll figure that out later," he replies, slipping the ring on my left hand.

Finally, I hear the words I both dread and anticipate. "You may kiss the bride."

Turner removes his cowboy hat, leaning in to peck my lips. He quickly pulls back, his eyes darting from my face to the justice's.

Behind us, the construction worker laughs and says, "You kiss the way you accuse me of tiling floors. Half-assed."

Turner shoots daggers at him before capturing me around the waist. To my surprise, he leans me off balance, sweeping me back and planting his lips firmly on mine. I'm so shocked that I exclaim, "Oh!"

Whether instinctively or because he misreads my parted lips, the burly cowboy claims my mouth. The gesture sends hungry waves of desire through me as his velvety, wet tongue strokes mine, pulling a deep moan from me. *God, this man can kiss!*

I wrap my arms around his neck, letting the bouquet waterfall to the ground. My heart thrums in my head as he explores my mouth, and I return the favor, sinking into his irresistible taste and feel. Pure, delicious masculine possessiveness.

Straightening me back up, he pulls away, and I can only describe the look on his face as disturbed.

Does he think I'm a terrible kisser? If so, that's news to me.

The judge declares, "I now have the pleasure of introducing Mr. and Mrs. Turner West."

The construction worker congratulates, "That's more like it."

I lean down, happy to focus on the fallen flowers rather than look into my new husband's eyes. I'm not used to being bashful, but this day has been too much. The last thing I woke up thinking this morning was that I'd lose my home, lose my siblings, and gain a husband all before noon. I straighten back up, and Turner grabs my hand, his face a dark storm.

Leaning down, he whispers in my ear. "Sorry about the kiss. But I'd never hear the end of it on the construction site after that challenge."

"I'm not sorry," I blurt out before thinking, and a surprised smile crosses the handsome cowboy's face as he lets go of my hand to thread his arm around my waist.

"Well, alright then..." he replies. He grips my waist and hip possessively, and I feel flames beneath his fingers. Thank goodness for the dress because I think skin-to-skin contact with this man in this area of my body would burn me alive.

Justice Powell has paperwork for us to sign, followed by the tiler. After everything's legal and in order, Turner commands, "Grab your coat, Strawberry. It's time to get your family back."

Chapter Twelve

TURNER

I s God trying to punish me for past sins? Or teach me a lesson about self-control? If so, I have to hand it to Him for finding a doozy of a way to torture and tempt me simultaneously.

Ever since she moved to Rough & Ready, the sight of Lily Monroe has fucked me up. I want her so badly that it makes my mouth dry and my throat knot. And that's nothing compared to what she does to me from the neck down.

Over the past three months, the only thing that has helped are distance and distraction. But without the first barrier, I have to double down on the distraction side of things. *Will that be enough with both of us under the same roof?*

As I stared into her eyes, saying vows I thought I'd never say to anyone, something happened to my heart. It came back to life in ways I didn't think possible, resurrecting hopes and expectations I thought I'd long ago laid to rest. But this renewed tenderness comes with a consequence I won't tolerate —vulnerability. I remind myself this is a marriage of convenience.

Besides, women may work out for some men, but they've

always disappointed me. Hell, more than disappointed me—broken my fucking heart and left me in shattered pieces. And it all started with my artsy, idealistic mother who was both too good for this world and a solid reflection of its shortcomings.

Lily reminds me too much of her. Now that she wears Mama's ring on her finger, I feel more conflicted than ever. All I know is I can't let my shield down with this woman, no matter what. If I start trusting her, showing my softer side, she'll eviscerate me. It's just a matter of time.

At the truck, I open the door and boost the pretty redhead into the seat. Then, I shake hands with the tiler. "Thanks for stepping up on such short notice." I should leave it there. But I'm feeling morose and pissed. So, I add, "You need to find a new day job. You're no professional tiler."

The man shrugs. "I'm good enough for Hutton and Smith."

"I imagine you are, so stick with tract homes. I don't want to see you on another of my projects. Got it?"

The man nods, looking down dejectedly. "You're in for one hell of a marriage with that smoking hot little number. Good luck keeping her satisfied and loyal," he says, turning to walk away. "Just remember, Karma's a bitch."

"If you're such good friends with Karma why don't you tell that bitch to teach you how to tile," I grumble, rounding the truck to get in.

I hear him yell back, "Asshole!"

In the truck, I mutter, "What a fucking loser."

Lily doesn't look at me. Instead, she's got her head in her hands, sobbing. *Is it really that bad being married to me?* We're less than fifteen minutes in, and she's a mess.

I scold, "You've got to pull yourself together, girl. We need to go into Social Services as a united front. And you need to convince Darlene and her supervisor that you *happily* married me. So, woman up or whatever you chicks say."

"Woman up?" she half sobs, half chuckles, wiping fat teardrops from her cheeks.

I count the subtle change in mood as a victory. Etiquette tells me I should inquire about why she cries. But the last thing I need is a rundown of flaws from my wife. Fake or not, her words would cut me.

I turn up the radio to fight the awkwardness of the car ride. We listen to classic rock, and I'm surprised to hear Lily singing along to Lynyrd Skynyrd, Heart, and Pink Floyd.

"This music's awfully old for a young thing like you."

"What's your weird obsession with my age? It seems to be the only thing you can talk about."

I don't feel like psychoanalyzing my hangups. As a foster kid with an abusive and traumatic past, I logged far more hours in therapist offices before the age of eighteen than I care to admit. "I'm just trying to make conversation with you. You don't have to get so defensive."

"I'm not getting defensive," she counters. "But you bring it up in nearly every conversation we have. Isn't there a pretty big age gap between your foster brother, Flynn, and his girl, Jasmine?"

Her words startle me, and I bark back, "How do you know Flynn and Jasmine?"

She replies, "I heard you on the phone earlier talking to Flynn and calling him 'brother.' In a town of two thousand, I'm guessing there can't be more than one, and he comes in regularly to the Silver Fork with Jasmine. I know she can't be much older than me."

"She isn't," I reply. "But that doesn't mean anything."

"But isn't Flynn around your age?"

I shrug, feeling like she's questioning me into a trap. "He's thirty-one. What's your point?"

"I'm not trying to make a point. I'm just trying to understand where you're coming from. So, are you opposed to them being together?"

I shake my head. "Not at all. They're perfect together."

She laughs, "So if you were thirty-one, things would be okay?"

"I see where you're trying to go with this, Lily, but it's comparing apples to oranges."

"From what you're telling me, you're the problem, not me. It's not that I'm too young. It's that you're too old," she triumphantly says as we pull into the Social Services parking lot.

Lily has a point, but I don't feel like admitting it. Instead, I say, "This whole conversation is irrelevant. After all, this marriage is fake, right?"

"Of course," she sputters, looking annoyed.

"Alright, then."

"But can you at least quit calling me 'girl' and talking about my age all of the time? Quite frankly, it's patronizing and demeaning. I may be young by your standards, but I'm well-educated and have fully formed opinions. I've probably done enough thinking and analyzing for people twice my age, and most people who know me consider me an old soul."

"The boring old guy and the old soul... We're perfect for each other," I mutter.

"I wouldn't go that far." She chuckles, looking up at the menacing building. Lily's countenance pales as her eyes wander to the black SUV that left earlier from the Monroe place with her siblings. I know that look because I've seen it reflected back at me many times. She's reliving traumatic memories.

I grab Lily's hand and kiss it gently. A surprised look crosses her face, and I explain, "It's time to quit fighting like an old married couple and start acting a little more like newlyweds. Are you ready to prove to Darlene and the good folks at

CPS that our little arrangement is more than convenient...or neighborly?"

"Whatever it takes to get my siblings back," she replies, forcing the corners of her mouth to go up on the sides. "Oh, and Turner, I need to say this now before this goes any further. I can't begin to express my appreciation for what you did at the house today and then at the courthouse. I don't understand why. I mean, don't you hate me?"

She couldn't be further from the truth, but she doesn't need to know this. "I don't hate you, and I never have. But our personalities are all wrong for each other. That's all..." My voice trails off.

Somehow, it feels like I'm lying again, and I don't understand why.

The redhead asks, "Why are you doing this, and what do you want from me in return?"

A cold sweat breaks out on my forehead. This woman needs to quit asking me what I want, or one of these days, I might show her. I say, "Perhaps I'm trying to right a past wrong."

"Which past wrong?" she whispers.

I grumble, "Maybe someday I'll tell you." But in my heart of hearts, I sincerely doubt it.

In my experience with women, sharing sad childhood stories never leads anywhere good. Sure, it might make a woman pity me for a while or put up with my shit for longer than she should. But eventually, it all goes south.

I imagine this would be especially true considering Lily's upbringing. She had two parents that loved and cared for her. How could she begin to understand my shitty youth? Or why it still haunts me to this day?

A knock on my car window startles me. Whipping around, I see Christian with a grimace on his face and his hands crossed over his chest. He looks in no mood to deal with my shit.

In my youth, his stance and expression would've sent me running to the edge of the ranch to avoid a whooping. Now, it elicits an entirely different response from me.

Getting out, I hug him, and he smacks me hard in the center of my back. "I don't know what the fuck you think you're doing," he grumbles. "But I'm here to provide backup and hopefully prevent you from losing your mind."

"Too late," I reply, the corners of my mouth turning down.

"What do you mean?" Christian asks, tensing his jaw.

"Lily and I just came from the courthouse where we tied the knot."

"What in the hell is going on, little bro?"

Lily rounds the side of the truck to stand next to me. She wraps her arms around herself, staring at the Social Services building. Her face looks ashen.

"Lily from the Silver Fork," my brother says, and she nods. But her expression is somber and her eyes filled with worry.

"Nice to see you again, Sheriff," she squeaks.

Rubbing my hand over my heart, I say, "I'll explain everything later. I don't want you getting involved, especially if you think it could impact your re-election campaign later."

The blond, clean-shaven sheriff wearing a crisp tan-and-black uniform shakes his head. "I don't worry too much about shit like that. I just try to do what's right—"

"And that's what I'm trying to do," I butt in.

"Yeah, but it's a lot to comprehend. Especially since you've spent the last three months complaining about how hot the neighbor girl is and how you're doing everything in your power to avoid her."

Motherfucker. He had to go and say that.

Lily's face reddens, and she laughs. Her gaze bobbles back

and forth between us as she says matter-of-factly, "Obviously, he finally quit avoiding me."

Christian's face clouds, and he stares down at the ground. He says, "So that you know, I have very little say over family court matters."

"We're not going to let it get that far," I reply, grabbing Lily's hand. I've got the paperwork in my other.

It's nearly one o'clock when we check in and sit in the waiting room next to my lawyer, Hobbes. He fills me in on his most recent conversation with Darlene and her supervisor. Within five minutes, the front receptionist ushers us back into a small room with tables and chairs.

Chapter Thirteen

TURNER

Darlene enters with her supervisor, Rudolph Telemann. I've met him several times at networking events and charitable giving organizations. As soon as he looks at me, he knows I've got his balls in my pocket.

West Homes gives a sizable annual donation to Social Services for the foster children's Christmas party. Perhaps I'm operating in a morally gray area. But now that Lily and I are married, I can honestly assure him of one thing. The Monroe children will be safe and supervised at all times.

I relish plopping the marriage paperwork down in front of Darlene and watching her as she makes a show of pouring over it before passing it to Rudolph. He barely glances at it. Christian stands behind us, quiet and imposing. Between my lawyer, my status in this county, and having the sheriff on-site and on our side, the outcome is obvious.

But Lily still looks panic-stricken. She twists her hands in her lap, a pained expression on her face until I can't take it anymore. Grabbing her left hand with my right, I give her a confident nod and smile. Her entire body relaxes, and I relish my ability to reassure and comfort her.

"I don't mean to rush this, but time's wasting," Christian butts in. "I've got a wife to get home to, and this couple's got kids to get to bed and a marriage to celebrate. Can we speed up the reunion already?"

Darlene's face looks livid. My guess is she never expected me to call her bluff. But Rudolph orders her, "Go get the Monroe children. There's no reason to keep them in custody any longer."

She nods, looking down as she walks past, and Lily squeezes my hand, flashing me an ear-to-ear grin. It's like sunshine after a rainstorm, warming me from the inside out. As crazy as my plan has been, her face lets me know I've done the right thing.

Rudolph addresses me, "Expect us to touch bases with you to see how the children are doing sometime this next week. What's your address?"

I pull out my wallet and hand him my driver's license.

The door opens, and the children rush in, crashing into their sister like a defensive line piling on top of a quarterback.

Christian squeezes my shoulder, and I look up at him. His face is rigid, but a warmth in his eyes lets me know he gets what I'm doing, at least on some level.

Clapping his hands, Christian declares, "Alright, folks, let's get this show on the road. You guys can hug and make up when you get home."

The children reluctantly let their older sister go, and she turns to me, gratitude radiating from her face. Her hands come up to my cheeks, and before I can react, she leans in, kissing me. It's an innocent peck compared to the last one. I wonder whether our audience or her boundaries have more to do with that. But it still gets my blood pumping, inspiring me to want impossible things, because she initiated.

"Are you done with us, Rudolph?" I ask, leveling my gaze on him.

He nods, handing my driver's license back to me. "We'll be in touch, Mr. West." Standing, he leans over the desk to shake my hand and Lily's. "Congratulations to you both, and my sincere apologies for this misunderstanding." He shoots one more nervous look in my direction.

I nod firmly, narrowing my eyes at him and letting my frown soften slightly. Darlene conveniently stands in the hallway, refusing to make eye contact as we pass.

Hobbes comes up next to me. I pat him on the back, thanking him. "That went much smoother than I expected. Nice work."

The lawyer smiles smugly, holding the paperwork we received from the courthouse. "Incremental pressure always does the trick. Although I must say, the sheriff was a nice touch. Would you like me to file these with the rest of your important documents?"

I nod.

"Oh, and shall I start working on Ms. Monroe's last name change?"

The question takes me aback, and I glance questioningly towards Lily. She nods hesitantly.

The redhead looks just as surprised as I feel, but I remind myself we're not out of the woods yet. "Yes, Hobbes, that would be much appreciated."

Lily West. It has a nice ring to it...

What the fuck are you thinking, Turner? This is a fake marriage.

At the truck, Lily works on piling the kids in and buckling their seat belts. We don't have enough room for everyone, so Christian offers to take two. Cole and Poppy jump at the chance to ride in a real cop car, making the decision easy.

I dismiss Hobbes with another thank you while Lily climbs in the passenger seat. Minutes later, we're on the way back to Hollister.

Jack holds Lily's hand over the seat. The shy boy with coppery hair and gray-blue eyes doesn't say much beyond, "I missed you" and "I was scared." But joy and relief are written on his face.

Rosie won't stop talking a mile a minute, the polar opposite of her twin. Her curly, burgundy locks shake, and her turquoise eyes snap, as she confesses, "It was so scary. I thought I'd never see you again, Sissy."

Lily fights back tears as she offers her little sister her other hand. "You don't ever have to worry about us being separated again, thanks to Mr. West."

"The kids should call me Turner," I butt in. My mind's already fast-forwarding to the visits we'll get from CPS. Everything has to be in order and on the up and up.

"You're right," Lily says breathlessly, looking at me.

Daisy stays quiet in the back as Rosie relives the entire day, from the fire in the house to the car ride to Ophir City and getting to see real-life firefighters and the sheriff. Of all of the children, Daisy looks the most like her sister, Lily. But she has burgundy hair, sweeping eyebrows, and indigo eyes.

As we turn onto four eighty-eight, nearing my cabin, Daisy says, "Darlene kept asking me how long you and Turner have been dating. And she wanted to know if you ever shared a bedroom."

"What?" Lily questions, her voice shaking and her face going bright red. I've been around her enough to know this is pure anger rather than embarrassment.

Shit. It puts a severe kink in the sleeping arrangements I had planned, with the redhead taking my master bedroom and me sleeping in the guest bedroom.

"What did you tell her?" Lily asks, glancing over her shoulder at Daisy.

The adolescent shrugs. "I told Darlene it was none of her business and to leave me alone."

Lily's face relaxes.

Daisy asks guiltily, "Did I say something wrong?"

Lily's mouth opens, but no words come out. I can see she's working hard to find the best answer.

I butt in, saying, "Daisy, you should always show respect to authority figures. But yes, under the circumstances, what you said was perfect. Good job."

"Why is he talking to me like Dad used to?" she says, speaking to her sister as if I'm not in ear range. There's a sassy edge to her voice that I don't care for.

I grumble, "Because you're living under my roof now. That means I deserve and demand the respect of an authority figure. And the same goes for your sister. You will respect and obey us. You understand?"

Three pairs of eyes round as they nod.

"Good. I hope that's the first and the last time we need to have this talk."

Lily intervenes. "They're just kids, and they've had a hard day."

I side-eye her. "You may not like this, Lily, but I won't allow your siblings to walk all over you. You've sacrificed everything for them, and they will understand you deserve respect. You're my wife, fictional or not, and I won't allow bad-mannered behavior. No matter what."

Lily shakes her head, looking at me frantically. I frown, wondering what she thinks I said wrong.

"What's fit-shun-all mean?" Rosie pipes up.

The question hits me like a ton of bricks. Shit, these kids are listening to everything I say.

Daisy frowns. "It means not real."

An icy quiet fills the cab as I kick myself for my unfiltered words. Lily leans in, her mouth no more than an inch from my ear. She whispers, "Kids repeat everything they hear and see. So, we need to be more careful."

The heat of her breath on my ear makes my cock twinge. Guiltily, I shift the way I sit to ease the pressure from my Wranglers.

I break into a cold sweat, only finally realizing the magnitude of what I've done. It was one thing to get fake married and then plan on keeping my distance. But if we've got to pretend twenty-four-seven that we're actual newlyweds with five pairs of eyes and ears documenting our every move... Well, all bets are off.

Trepidation floods me as I glance at the scarlet-hued beauty next to me. Lily takes my hand, making sure the kids see her action.

Delicious tendrils of desire snake up my arm at her soft touch, and our eyes lock for the briefest moment before I return my attention to the road. I let out a long exhale, trying to focus on driving rather than every naughty thing I'd love to do to my neighbor.

Would it be so bad if I pleasured my wife? Or maybe even fell in love with her? I don't know where these rogue thoughts come from, but I find myself caressing her hand sensually. Trying to put in my touch the lovemaking that's on my mind.

She smiles, side-eyeing me, her cheeks scarlet, her fingers returning and intensifying my need. The look on her face lets me know this angel's thinking anything but heavenly thoughts. I swallow loudly, adjusting how I sit yet again.

Shit and fuck. This marriage just became more real than when I slipped my mother's ring on Lily's finger. And if I'm being honest, I want to do a whole lot more than play house with my pretend wife.

Clearing my throat, I try hard to get back to the business at hand. "We'll stop by your house on the way to the cabin. That way, you can pack up what you need for the night and get Trix's food and water bowls and whatever else you need for him."

"Thank you," she replies. "And I'll get your wedding band..."

My brows knit.

"It was my dad's, but I think it'll fit."

I shake my head. "No, Lily, I can't let you do that."

"If it's too macabre for you, I get it. But otherwise, seeing it on your hand would comfort me."

"In that case, I'll wear it," I reply, torn about every part of this day.

Chapter Fourteen

LILY

My heart sinks into my stomach as I walk through the front door of my neighbor-turned-husband's cabin, and my jaw hangs on the ground. Everything is immaculate, clutter-free, and expensive.

I survey the vaulted ceilings with skylights, bathing the interior in golden sunshine. Huge windows ensure breathtaking views of the mountains and forest, and a massive hearth made from local granite gives the place a rugged, cozy feel. Everything about this place feels like home and has me rethinking my dislike of the Sierra Nevada backcountry.

After all, where could I find these views and this coziness in a big city like Paris? It wouldn't be possible. And I know many of my Parisian friends would give anything to swap places with me, not only location-wise but for a chance with this impossibly handsome cowboy.

Do I have a chance with him, though?

Based on how he looked at me and caressed my hand on the way home from Ophir City, I'd say "yes." But pesky thoughts linger about how he's treated me for the past three months. Never has a person made his desire to avoid me more clear. However, in the context of what his brother, Christian, said, it makes sense. My head spins, trying to figure out what all of this means...and why I feel irresistibly and irrepressibly drawn to him, like a moth to a flame.

I shake my head, looking around to clear my mind. The furniture is handmade and one-of-a-kind. The sophistication of the decor impresses me, making me reconsider my long-standing assessment that he's an uncouth redneck.

My eyes fall on the spotless white couch cushions accented with Native American patterned blankets and pillows, and my pulse races. I know what my sisters and brothers are capable of. They could destroy this place in half an afternoon.

The only non-destructible part of Turner's cabin is the wood flooring, stained in a rich cedar color. I open my mouth to lay down the law, but the handsome mountain man beats me to the punch line.

"No eating or drinking anywhere but at the dining room table. Always take your shoes off and leave them by the front door. No silly string, silly putty, slime, or any other substance that could stain my couches. And honestly, while we're on the subject of the couches, don't go anywhere near them...under any circumstances." He glares at me. "That goes for Trix, too."

I swallow loudly, looking around. The man still has no idea what he's gotten himself into. I add, "No touching the walls." They're a perfect shade of off-white with brown accents that do not need children's greasy handprints. "Don't touch anything..." I shake my head, looking around, over-whelmed.

Delicate metal sculptures sit on the mantle and the coffee table, drawing my attention. An eye trained by years of art study lets me know these are one-of-a-kind objects.

"Where did you get these?" I ask, stepping forward to finger the statue of a voluptuous goddess with locks flowing to her waist.

Turner's face is stone. "Why are you asking?"

I pull my hand back, covering my mouth. "I'm sorry. I shouldn't have touched her. She's...she's just so stunning. They all are." I motion towards the other metal sculptures. "I've never seen an artist bring metal to such fluid life like this before. It's almost like I can feel her breathing, see her moving...feel the passions igniting her from the inside out."

He lets out a long sigh. "You like her?" he asks, his eyes narrowing and his face storming.

"I love her. I love all of them. These are the kind of sculptures I want to sell someday when I have my own art gallery."

Sincere pleasure lights up his face, but he tempers it, gruffly muttering, "So you approve of my taste in art?"

I nod emphatically.

He offers, "Maybe I could arrange for you to meet the artist some day."

"Really?"

"Really," he says, looking away and tugging at the collar of his button-down shirt.

I continue, "And your wall art, too. Yes, I wholeheartedly approve."

Light, airy canvases hang on his walls. Inspired by the Post-Impressionists and Expressionists, I make a mental note to ask him more about their creators later.

A stack of abstract art books sits on the small table in front of the couch. Never in a million years did I see this coming from my grumpy old neighbor. Eyeing more one-of-a-kind paintings, I can imagine how much they cost, and it makes me tremble. His cabin looks more like a modern art museum than a residence. There's no way this home will survive my siblings.

I head towards one of the pieces hanging on his living room wall. It's a gorgeous, gaudy mixture of color and texture that feels like a celebration. Not something I'd expect decorating the home of a staid cowboy.

He stands shoulder-to-shoulder with me, and I savor the warm, spicy cologne he wears. "I got this a couple of years ago from an artist I met at Burning Man, Vince Lowell."

"You go to Burning Man?" I ask, floored.

"Every year," he replies with a steely gaze. "I want to see your artwork, too, Lily. When you feel ready to show me." The invitation both thrills and terrifies me.

I sputter, "No way. Not with taste like this. You'll think I'm an amateur."

His baby blues drill into me, and his jaw tenses. "I doubt that—"

The chaos of children indoors interrupts the man mid-sentence.

Shaking my head, I turn towards the kids, ordering, "Put your coats back on and go outside this instant. Take Trix with you."

Despite everything that happened today, a couple of hours of sunlight remain. I want to take full advantage of this time to let the kids run off some of their energy.

They've already made a coat pile on the floor by the door, and I can see the surprised look on Turner's face as he takes it in. The commotion of them digging through the heap and putting on their respective garments gives way to scrambling back through the front door with the dog and then silence.

My eyes settle more closely on the coffee table I glanced at when first entering the home. As I stare at the immaculate lines and folk art details, my eyes fill with tears. I discreetly wipe my wet cheeks with the back of my hand, but it's too late.

Turner grips my shoulders with his hands, keeping a whole arm's length of distance between us. "Why are you crying?"

I shake my head, looking away. He doesn't need to see me like this. In fact, he needs to mind his own business.

A firm finger snags me under the chin, forcing my eyes towards his. In a softer voice, he repeats, "Why are you crying?"

A sob grips me at the question, and all I can manage is: "The coffee table."

His brows furrow, and his eyes stray toward the furniture before recognition lights up his face. He frowns, nodding his head. "Your dad built that. Yes..."

I look down again, shaking my head. "I'm sorry. I should be stronger than this."

"Losing a parent is never easy." His voice has a rawness to it I've never heard before. "And I can't imagine what it'd be like to lose two at the same time."

I shrug. "It's life, right? Nobody said it would be fair. I just miss them..." Waves of sorrow crash into me now, and Turner hesitantly pulls me into his arms. I notice how careful he is to keep a few inches of distance between our bodies.

"My mom's been dead for years now," he says, resting his chin on top of my head while he gently strokes my hair with his hand. "But I still have trouble with the whole thing... And I miss her, too."

"What happened to her?" I ask quietly, feeling his body immediately stiffen. I've gotten too personal. I open my mouth to apologize for the question, but his deep, grumbly voice cuts me off.

"I don't want to talk about it." He pulls back, putting distance between us again. My body immediately misses his warmth and comfort. "Enough of the fucking heart-to-hearts. You've got kids to watch, and I've got to figure out what it will take to get your cabin back in working order again. While we're on the subject of your siblings, there's one more rule I forgot to mention. Under no circumstances are any of them allowed near my workshop. Do you hear me?"

He ends so many of his sentences with "you understand?,"

"do you hear me?," or some variation of these questions. It feels like he's talking down to me. I think this is part of what made me assume he was much older than he is. Between the rhetorical questions and the "girl" talk, he couldn't make his contempt for me more evident.

Turner looks down. "Next order of business. You need to turn in your notices at work."

I nod, already resigned that he doesn't want me at the gas station or Stonie's.

"That includes the Silver Fork."

"Why the Silver Fork?" I ask, surprised and irritated by his commanding tone.

"Because there's no way in hell any of your siblings can go unsupervised in my house. And no wife of mine would work at a place like that."

"So, it's good enough to eat at with your clients? But not good enough for me to work at?"

His eyes drill into me, and he replies through gritted teeth, "I refuse to have guys ogling you all morning long. It's the last thing I'd let my wife do, and since you're temporarily filling that spot, it's the last thing you'll do."

"Are you still upset about my excuse to Darlene for not wearing an engagement ring?" I ask. "It was the only thing I could think of."

He looks floored by the question. "Was I upset in the first place?"

I raise my eyebrows, nodding hesitantly. There's much I still have to learn about my neighbor. But I have a pretty good handle on when he's pissed at me.

He relents, confessing, "Alright, I admit it made me sound like a loser and a moron."

I'm surprised by the insecurity in his voice, realizing I've hit him in the ego. My mom always warned me that a man never forgives having his ego attacked. So, I drop the subject without another word.

But he's not done. "My brother isn't buying this situation as it is, and neither is Darlene. The only way to convince my family and this town is to treat you like I would...you know, the real deal." His cheeks darken at the last statement, and he looks away, adding as an afterthought, "Don't you have your art history studies or something to get back to, anyway?"

A thousand emotions pulse through me at his words. To my utter astonishment, something about his jealousy and possessiveness is a total turn-on. But the sarcasm in Turner's voice as he pronounces "art history" jolts me unceremoniously from my reverie.

"Do you think art history is a frivolous study?" I ask.

"It's a good way to end up homeless," he growls. "But you don't have to worry about that anymore...now that you've got a millionaire wrapped around your finger."

Staring at him, I feel frustrated. I can't read his face to decide whether he's joking or speaking from more insecurity. I won't let him think I'm a gold digger, though.

Raising my chin defiantly, I reply, "I'd rather be homeless than take help from anybody, and as for marrying for money? That's despicable."

"But marrying on false pretenses? You're okay with?"

"Marrying for love is what I'm okay with." I mean, marrying for the love of my siblings, but the words come out all wrong.

The cowboy's eyes narrow, and the Adam's apple in his neck jumps as he swallows. A strange expression captures his face before recognition slams into him. "You mean the love of your siblings... I see."

I nod, but my face blazes. Turner's jaw tightens, and he says quietly, "Your siblings are lucky to have you, Lily." Then, he turns on his heel and walks away.

Chapter Fifteen

TURNER

A *boring old guy...* I can't get Lily's words out of my head. I sit at the kitchen counter, twirling the wedding band on my left hand. It feels strange on my finger, and I wonder what Donovan Monroe would say about it...

After knocking me out cold for marrying his baby girl, I suppose he'd tell me to take care of her and his kids. And I could do that...

Maybe better than any man in this damn town...

If I could shake the guilt I feel about her age. Or the trepidation about her lack of life experience. At thirty-four, I'm finally at the age where I know what I want. How can I expect the same from a twenty-one-year-old woman?

But if I keep pushing her away...making her wait, I could lose any shot with her forever. And can I really stand the thought of another man stepping in to fill the void I refuse to occupy? Especially knowing what fuck-tards guys her age are? Doing the right thing never felt so confusing or unclear.

My biggest fear is that, eventually, she'll tire of me. Find a newer and shinier model. Or move back to Paris. Maybe that's why the "boring old guy" comment hit so close to home. Because I already fear I'll never be able to keep the one woman I want so badly I can feel it in the marrow of my bones.

My eyes drop to the large black portfolio she handed me before heading to bed. It contains her most portable artwork. She said most of her canvases still sit in Paris at her advisor's house because she didn't have time to dismantle and roll them before racing home.

She's got an incredible gift when it comes to realistic portraits. I can see the spark in her subject's eyes—flesh, blood, and emotion fully conveyed. And her use of color and shading are both noteworthy. Pastels, charcoal, colored pencils... Her skill in different media is apparent, even though she prefers oil paint.

But even more than the skill of her renderings is the intense energy behind them... the swirl of passion pulling them off the page. They speak to my soul in a way I can't explain and never saw coming.

Fuck, I'm in trouble. Deep trouble.

I couldn't lie in bed with her tonight after the kids went to sleep. Sure, I've got a California King, and we should be able to keep a reasonable distance between us. But my mind keeps racing, and my body's got its own wants.

I've never lacked self-control. But something external compels me towards Lily. As if we're twin flames, inexorably drawn together... While I understand the strange preciousness of these unprecedented feelings, can she? At little more than twenty-one? Thinking back to the early twenties version of myself, I doubt it.

Shaking my head, I scan the darkened room to clear my mind. A pink spot on my favorite area rug attests to the spaghetti six-year-old Jack accidentally dropped during dinner. Muddy paw prints line the living room, courtesy of Trix. And a pile of rejected blankets reminds me of the nighttime drama when Daisy couldn't find her favorite blanket and burst into frantic sobs. So, we had to make the trek next door to retrieve hers.

Lily kept her siblings wrangled outside until the mid-February weather quit cooperating, and they had to come in. I can't expect it to hold out forever, though. We often get our worst snowstorms in March. Sometimes, even in April.

I sigh, thinking about that bunch of ruffians tearing through my house. That's what I get for paying it forward, or what the fuck ever I thought I was doing when I contrived this whole fake marriage thing.

Warm milk heats in a saucepan on the stove, and I close the portfolio, pushing it back onto the counter. I can't look at her artwork anymore.

Three months of inconsolable longing and desire torment me. And the chaste (and not so chaste) kisses we shared today continue to incinerate me, lighter fluid to open flames.

If it was merely a lust thing, I could get it under control. No problem. But I don't just want her with my body. I want her with my soul. Appreciating her artwork painfully confirms this truth.

She's a professionally trained artist, and you're just a hobby sculptor. Don't get ahead of yourself, Turner.

I open my phone, reading the messages I've avoided all afternoon. One brother after another has texted me, informed by Christian and his wife, Cricket, of my unexpected nuptials and instant family. Some, like Logan, Zane, and Wolfe, are angry because I haven't kept them in the loop.

What the fuck ever. I'm certainly not on speed dial when it comes to their love lives, either. But, oddly enough, Flynn is the most surprised, even though I consulted him in advance. His text reads:

"I know what we discussed on the phone this morning.

But I still can't believe you went through with it. Wtf?!?! Did you have to beat me to the altar, too?"

I can't help but chuckle at the message sprinkled with emojis. Ever since he got into a relationship with Jasmine, he's started using them more. I feel like she must've given him a tutorial at some point.

Flynn and I have always had a healthy rivalry. But I can earnestly say that the one thing I wasn't trying to outdo him on is commitment. Too late now, though...

It's past three in the morning, so my return text to him will have to wait. As for my younger brothers, Maksim and Travis, they don't act nearly as butt-hurt by my lack of keeping them in the loop.

Maksim has little room to talk, considering he fell in love with a girl in less than a week after saving her from a blizzard. Talk about crazy. And Travis, always the firefighter, shows more concern about what happened at Lily's house today.

"Kurt told me about the incident at the Monroe house. Is everyone okay? Glad to hear there wasn't significant structural damage."

But the kicker comes from Logan. His wife, Jess, has decided that she and my other sisters-in-law are taking Lily out for a day of post-wedding pampering.

Post-wedding pampering? The word "wedding" in my context continues to startle me. I still can't wrap my head around how everything went down...

Trix rustles in his metal crate in the corner of the living room, and almost-silent footfalls sound in my direction.

Great! *Which fucking kid am I going to have to entertain tonight?*

I glance over my shoulder, and my heart stops. Lily stands in the entryway between the living room and the kitchen, wide-eyed and open-mouthed. Her eyebrows rest at the top of her forehead, and she acts like my presence in the kitchen is unexpected, even though it's *my own damn house.*

Her hand comes to her chest, and I take longer than I should, appreciating the silky emerald green robe that falls midway down her shapely calves. The teasing flash of green lace poking out at the front where the tie holds it closed tantalizes my imagination.

Fuck, what I wouldn't give to unwrap such a mouthwatering package. One thing's for sure. She would never fucking regret it, and she'd stop referring to me as a boring old guy.

I rub the spot over my heart absent-mindedly before registering the fact her hungry eyes are devouring every inch of my bare chest, all the way down to the waistband of my red-and-navy plaid flannel pajama pants. Her eyes dilate, and her cheeks redden. It takes every ounce of my willpower not to stride in her direction, wrap my arms around her, and claim her with a soulful kiss.

Swallowing loudly, I work hard to get my brain going again to speak. "What are you doing up, Strawberry?" Thankfully, my pants fit loosely, or she'd get an eyeful of the action she inspires below the belt.

I hear her swallow, too, and she licks her lips slowly, still shamelessly drinking me in with her eyes. "I saw the light on and thought one of the kids was up."

I see right through her excuse. She had to realize it was me the moment she turned on the bedroom light and noticed my absence. But if it makes her feel more comfortable about the situation, I'll give it to her. Instead, I ask, "Are you having trouble sleeping?"

She nods.

"Would you like some warm milk? It always does the trick for me."

She bites her lower lip, and her eyes grow red with tears. It feels like everything I say ends with her crying. Being emotional shouldn't surprise me under the circumstances, but it's still starting to fuck with my mind...making me hesitant to speak.

"Hey, what's wrong?" I ask in soft tones, pulling out the stool next to me. I expect her to refuse it. But to my amazement, she sits, staring down at her hands and then back at me. Her lovely forest-hued eyes wander to my shoulders and chest again, and warm pride fills me. It's obvious she digs me.

"My mom used to warm milk for me when I couldn't sleep. I know everyone does it, and it shouldn't bother me. But..." She squeezes her lips tightly together, looking down at her hands.

My mind flashes through what to do. Should I lean forward and put my hand reassuringly over hers? Should I place a hand on her shoulder? Or should I draw her into my arms and lap, whispering comforting things in her ear? The last one is what I really want to do. After all, that's what a husband would do, right? Instead, I remain motionless, staring at the curvy goddess before me.

The way she twists her hands in agitation in her lap catches my attention. And at this closer distance, her puffy cheeks and lips tell me she's been crying for a while. She may be missing her mom, but there's far more to her current mood.

"What else, Lily?" I ask quietly.

"This morning, before learning about the fire, I gave up my place at art school. If you knew half of what I went through to get in... And I had to give up my scholarship, too. Compared to everything that happened today, I know it's nothing. But it still makes me sad."

"I understand where you're coming from," I say quietly. "When I was young and fresh out of high school, I had big city dreams, too. And ambitious educational goals. But when the opportunity to work for Broderick came up, my dad, Wyatt, wouldn't let me pass it up."

She listens raptly to my words, and there's nothing I wouldn't tell her at this moment. It's a terrifying thought as I continue baring my soul. "At the time, I felt angry about missed opportunities. But time and distance have shown me that taking the job with Broderick was the single best choice I've ever made. And working as a custom home builder is a passion in itself...one that doesn't preclude me from doing what I love on the weekends."

"In your workshop?" she adds.

I nod.

To my surprise, she asks, "What do you do in there?"

I shrug. "Maybe I'll show you sometime."

The mental exercise of tapping into my late teens and early twenties mindset lets me empathize with Lily without getting judgmental. It also brings me back to my original inclination. I shock myself as I motion for her to climb onto my lap and into my arms.

She freezes, her eyes as big as a doe's in headlights.

The awkwardness of the moment makes me insistent. "Come on, woman. I'm not going to bite you. And we might as well start practicing acting comfortable around each other. If you won't let me hold you...well, nobody's going to believe this is a real marriage."

Biting her lower lip, she nods, her face instantly red as she covers the distance between us, settling into my lap and arms. "I want you to hold me," she confesses quietly. "Your arms make me feel safe."

God, she feels good like this. Too damn good. And her words swell my heart, fortifying my resolve to make her happy at all costs. I just hope against all hope that her happiness will somehow involve me.

I can't doubt the woman's words because she melts into

me, making me feel like the most powerful man on the planet. I stroke her luscious locks, breathing in the smell of her hair— all juicy, fresh strawberries. I don't know what shampoo she uses, but I love it.

I croon gently in her ear, "I'm sorry about what happened, but you'll always be safe with me."

She wraps her arms around my neck, burying her head in my shoulder and sobbing. I savor the feel of her hot, wet cheeks on my naked shoulder, wishing I could absorb all of her sadness and bear it for her.

"That's right, Lily," I say softly, running my fingers through her silky locks. "From now on, I'm the one you come to when you feel this way. I'll be here for you no matter what."

She stiffens in my arms, and I wonder what I've said wrong now. Turning her head, she asks quietly, "Why are you doing all this for me? I mean, I've been nothing but a jerk to you."

"Because everybody needs somebody," I reply with conviction. "Especially when they're going through what you're going through. I know you don't know me well yet. But I'm not judgmental, and I won't ever hold things against you or break your confidence. I might be a boring old guy, but I have a heart..." I stop myself before I say something stupid. If I'm not careful, I could lose that heart to this girl at any moment.

Her head returns to my shoulder, and big, lusty sobs rock her until she slowly settles and relaxes in my arms. The feel of the slippery silk of her emerald robe and the warm, soft flesh beneath makes it hard to breathe, and my heart pounds behind my ribs. I wonder if she can feel it.

Of course, my cock wants more, so much more from this beautiful girl. But I would never take advantage of her when she's vulnerable like this. Having so much restraint feels bitter-sweet, though. Because one night with me would make her forget her troubles. At least temporarily.

She's too damn young for you, Turner, no matter how much you long to claim her as yours.

A rising column of steam and gurgling draw my attention to the stovetop. I don't want to let her go, but I need to remove the saucepan of milk from the heat before it scalds.

"Are you better?" I ask softly, and she nods her head.

"Alright, then. Have a seat, and I'll get you some warm milk."

Minutes later, we each have our hands around a warm mug. Lily stares into her steaming drink, and I gaze at her, trying to memorize everything about this moment. How the curtain of luxurious red locks waterfall around her face, the way her long lashes frame her hooded eyes, the alluring fullness of the lips I long to taste.

I've never felt this way about a woman in my life, and it scares the shit out of me. Because beyond the lust, there's so much more. A fierce need to protect her, a resolve to make her life better, an overriding curiosity about what makes her tick, what she loves, and how she sees the world.

"What are you staring at?" she asks breathlessly, meeting my gaze.

"You know what I'm staring at." Her cheeks glow, and I add, "I'm trying to understand you is all."

"There's not much to understand," she replies sadly.

"I know from our conversations and looking at your artwork that that's a lie," I challenge gruffly. "Tell me what made you fall in love with Paris." *Maybe there will be something in her answer that I can use to make her fall in love with me.*

Chapter Sixteen

TURNER

S he shakes her head, posing the question, "How to describe Paris?"

I wait patiently, worried that her response will underscore the hopelessness of my current situation. I've managed to fall for a much younger woman in love with a city rather than a flesh and blood man. What kind of an idiot do I have to be to think I can rival the "City of Lights"?

Passion illuminates her face as she says, "Paris is everything. It surges with a Bohemian energy that's kinetic. The artistic history of the city, the painters who have called it home, the museums, its aesthetic all spoke to my soul. Whether I was walking down the rain-soaked Champs-Elysées, holding my umbrella as impossibly chic pedestrians passed by, or savoring the decadent fragrance of freshly baked bread and pastries in the Metro."

"Freshly baked bread in the Metro?" I scrunch my face in confusion.

"Every afternoon, there's a time called goûter, which literally means 'to taste.' Think of it like an afternoon snack time for kids and adults. People pile into local bakeries for delectable treats—even in the Metro during their commute home. Maybe they'll have a simple croissant or something more wicked, like pain au chocolat—" The bewilderment on my face stops her mid-sentence.

"Pan what?" I repeat.

"Basically, a croissant with a chocolate center."

"Hmm...seems a little weird to me," I counter with a lopsided grin. "But I'd try it...I guess...with you."

She nods, smiling. "I thought the same thing until I moved there. But it's honestly yummy."

"Is that what you liked to eat each afternoon? Pan oh chocolate?"

She laughs at my lousy attempt at French. Shaking her head, she answers, "Not usually, although I had it every now and again when the bakery was sold out of my favorite treat, pain aux raisins."

"What's that?"

"It's kind of like a croissant stuffed with vanilla custard and topped with raisins and powdered sugar."

"That sounds similar to the almond croissants I used to get at this eclectic little bakery in Ophir City. But they stopped carrying them, which is a damn shame."

"Yes, croissant aux amandes in French. They have those at the bakeries, too."

"You know, Cricket, my brother Christian's wife owns the bakery in Hollister."

"Sweet Rush? Really? I adore that place!"

"Yeah, she's always looking for new treats to dazzle her clientele. If you want, I could put in a good word about some of those fancy French pastries you just described."

An ear-to-ear smile transforms her face, and I bask in the warmth of making her happy. It's like a drug. I can't get enough of pleasing her. It could become a lifelong pursuit if I'm not careful.

But this moment is too good to last. I can't keep opening myself up to this woman...like this. Our arrangement is temporary and pretend. The last thing I need is a fake broken heart because I got too caught up with a girl who still has to figure out who she is, let alone what kind of life and man she wants.

"You wouldn't do that for me," she replies flirtatiously.

Hell, yeah, I would. I nod firmly, running a hand through my brown hair. "There's not much I wouldn't do for you, Lily." The forthright confession shocks me even more than my scarlet-haired companion. I clear my throat awkwardly, grabbing my milk and taking a drink. *What the fuck was that?*

Lily's eyebrows are still in her hairline, and her eyes are large as she corners me, reminding me, "Your brother said you told him I'm hot. Did you really say that?"

I swallow hard, looking at her. *Fuck, I've never been a good liar. And especially not with convictions I feel in every bone and every cell of my body.* It's a lost cause, trying to be strategic with my words.

Instead, I blurt out, "Facts are facts, darling. Yeah, you're hot as fuck. But I doubt I'm the first man to tell you that."

She shrugs, looking away. I can't imagine how she could get this far in life without every guy on the planet fawning all over her. But the look on her face says otherwise. "I've never had much luck with men," she says flatly. "I don't know why, but I always attract users and losers. And as you can imagine, they don't stick around for long."

The stupidity of other men never ceases to amaze me. It's their loss. Besides, I don't want any other man's eyes on this woman. A fiercely possessive part of me wants to lock her up, keep all to myself like the world's most precious treasure. Because that's what she is, even if she doesn't know it.

My feelings embolden me. I inquire, "The question is, what do you think of me? I'd half think you liked what you saw earlier when you walked into the kitchen. Your eyes practically feasted on me. But there was that comment earlier that's still got me confused...'a boring old guy.' Which one is it?"

"Practically feasted on you? Okay, I never took you for egotistical. But you need to get over yourself already," she snaps back.

"Get over myself? It's a simple enough question." If it is, indeed, simple, why is my every hope riding on her answer?

Cocking her head to the side, she says, "I don't know."

"Don't know what? I asked you what you think of my looks. Am I your type?"

The last question elicits an irrepressible laugh. "My type? Absolutely not."

My stomach drops. "Why? Because I'm a hick, and I live in a small town rather than a big-ass city like Paris?"

"For starters."

"What else?" My eyes narrow.

"Well, you're not just a hick. You're a cowboy hat, boots, and buckle kind of hick, and you seem content living in a podunk little town where the most interesting thing that happens all day is found on a police scanner. Besides, you're not an artist, and I need to be with a fellow artist."

Ouch! She couldn't hurt me more if she grabbed a butcher knife and stabbed me in the chest. I open my mouth to speak but stop short.

I wish I knew her better. On the one hand, she looks like she's half teasing, half flirting with me. And she may very well be. But once I get my feelings hurt, moodiness follows. It's a Cancer thing.

Lamentably, she continues, "You're kind of uppity when it comes to things like working at a diner or a gas station, and you're super set in your ways. No offense, but I've always envisioned myself with a well-educated guy, too."

I clear my throat, feeling thoroughly gutted. "So, a blue-collar millionaire won't cut it?"

She exhales loudly. "I hate it when guys throw money around to impress a girl. I'm looking for a soulmate, not a paycheck."

I laugh darkly, "A soulmate...but only if he has a college degree... And I'm the one who's uppity?"

She opens her mouth to counter my argument, but nothing comes out.

"Well, as fun as this talk's been, I need to try to get some sleep tonight. It's getting light outside." I nod toward the kitchen window, where the purple of night is giving way to gorgeous periwinkle and pink swathes of color. "Don't worry. I'll sleep on the floor."

Her face looks somber. Like she finally realizes she's spent the last ten minutes insulting the hell out of me. This is what I get for letting myself fall for my neighbor. Of course, I never really had a choice.

"Are you done with your mug?" I ask icily, and she hands hers to me.

Looking down, the beauty bites her lower lip, setting my blood on fire. Shit, I need this woman out of my house. Like yesterday. "All jesting aside, I think you're hot as fuck, too," she admits.

"Do you now?" I ask, keeping my voice flat and disinterested. I don't know what game she's playing, but I want no part of it.

"I do."

"That's all fine and dandy. But honestly, honey, I could never be with someone as judgmental as you just proved yourself to be. So, I guess we're even."

"Judgmental?" Her face turns red with anger, but I'm done conversing with her. Instead, I focus on my exit plan.

I nod. "For someone who knows so little about me, you

sure act like you know an awful lot." I smile grimly. "Have a good night." I saunter past her, feeling her eyes devour me from behind.

"Turner," she calls after me.

I stop without turning around.

"What do you like about living in Rough & Ready Country? I've been trying to figure out what made my parents move here in the first place. Maybe you can help me answer that."

I glance over my shoulder, making my face as expressionless as possible. "Maybe an educated person like you could sum it up in words. But as for me, I'd have to show you."

Before she can answer, I nod curtly and stride towards the stairs.

Footfalls behind me let me know Lily is following me into the master bedroom. She watches me grab a pillow and blanket, preparing my floor bed.

"There's no way you're going to be comfortable like that. Just sleep on the bed next to me. We're both adults, after all." Her face looks determined as she adds, "Unless you don't think you have enough willpower to sleep next to a woman?"

I freeze, looking up at her. "Not enough willpower? I may be a hick, but I'm no caveman."

"Then, prove it," she replies.

This fucking woman. I frown, tossing the pillow back on the bed. "Whatever. All I know is I need a little shut-eye. Make sure you stay on your side of the bed, Ms. Monroe..."

"Mrs. West," she corrects, and I'm confounded. "And yes, I assure you I'll stay on my side."

Chapter Seventeen

LILY

I awaken slowly, feeling deliciously warm and safe. Turner's strong, muscular arms hold me against his rock-hard chest and stomach. His legs wrap lazily around mine, and I feel his large, granite-hard rod pressed against my back.

The relaxed pace of his breathing suggests he's still sleeping, but I can't tell for sure. My heart pounds against my chest, and I hold still, not ready to let go of this perfect moment.

At what point in the night did we end up this way? All I know is our bodies fit snugly together as if we were made for each other. I close my eyes, reveling in this unexpected intimacy. *Is this what it's like to have a husband?*

His right hand holds my breast, and I feel his fingers restlessly raking over my nipple barbell every now and again. This delicious motion must be what woke me up. His fingers play with it slowly, erratically, and I can't help myself.

I exhale, snuggling my hips and ass against his prominent cock. He sighs contentedly, pulling me more tightly against him and nestling his head in my hair.

God, he is awake! Or at least waking up, and he hasn't jumped out of bed or run from me.

This realization amplifies the throbbing between my legs until I'm ready to beg him to satisfy me. Nothing about this grumpy cowboy may be my type, but hell if that makes my body want him any less. And it isn't just lust that propels me towards him. It's the strange impression I've somehow found my way home.

"Your nipples are pierced," he says drowsily, starting to pull away, and my heart sinks. I grab his hand, placing it back on my breast and marveling at my assertiveness. He squeezes my tit confidently now, and his fingertips go from lightly brushing my nipple to actively stroking and teasing it until I hiss with desire.

What's gotten into you, Lily? I've never been like this with a man before. But I've also never hungered for a guy's touch like I thirst for Turner's. Lying together like this awakens a world of possibilities I never entertained until now, and they look more appealing and alluring by the minute. He snuggles into me some more, growling low in his throat.

That manly sound animates my entire body with desperate need. As if sensing this, he shifts so that his left arm, lying beneath my torso, finds my other nipple, amplifying the lust rising in my core.

"They are," I whisper, breathlessly. "Do you like them?" I squeeze my eyes shut, regretting the question and not sure I want to hear his answer.

"Hell, yeah," he says without hesitation, and a smile captures my lips. I realize I want him to want me...everything about me.

I close my eyes, savoring the feel of his rough, work-hardened hands as they continue to shower my breasts with attention before straying to my waist and hips, caressing and palming me. His body moves behind me sensually and seductively as he continues to wake up, and I want him inside of me more than anything.

It's the only thought thrumming through my brain, demanding and overwhelming. I bite my lower lip, willing his hands to travel lower. But they stay chastely clamped on my hips, even though his hands squeeze and knead my flesh with increasing fervor.

He nuzzles my neck, whispering, "I love how your hair smells." He buries his face in it, pressing tender kisses along my neck and shoulder until my body quakes with need.

"I should stop." The conflict in his voice couldn't be more apparent. Yet, he continues tasting and teasing my neck until shivers run from my fingers to my toes.

"Please, don't, Turner," I plead, marveling at the seductiveness of my voice. I've never heard it sound like this before, and I can't blame it all on early morning.

"I can't, Lily," he growls next to me. "There's only so much a man can take."

I swallow hard. "It's the same for a woman, you know."

The silence in the room feels heavy and thick.

"What do you mean?"

"I need you," I confess, grabbing his hand and moving it between my legs.

His body goes as stiff as his cock, and he groans, "No, Strawberry, don't tempt me with something I can't have." But his fingers find their way beneath my silky nightgown and into my underwear.

"You can have it," I say, swallowing hard. "I want you to."

"Are you sure?" His voice sounds raw and confused. Thinking back on how things ended last night, I can understand why. Honestly, I feel bewildered by my feelings, too.

But I need him. Every cell in my body, every inch of my flesh, cries out this demand. His hand cups my mound beneath my panties, his fingers unmoving. "If this isn't what you want, you need to stop me. Because making you happy is all I care about."

The tension of his hand so close to my pussy without actually touching me is too much. I can't take it. Through pants, I say, "I want you, Turner. More than I've ever wanted anyone."

The words surprise me, especially in the context of last night. But they're one hundred percent true. His fingers relax, and I moan as they slide through my folds. I spread my legs to encourage him, and he groans deep in his chest, sending delicious low vibrations through me.

His breath comes faster next to my ear, and he shifts so that the arm beneath me can get in on the action, too. "Yes," I sigh, melting into his skilled touch.

"Shh," he whispers, his voice dark and driven. "We don't want the kids to hear us."

His fingers slicken with my arousal as he runs them back and forth through my drenched folds. He groans against my hair, trying to stay quiet. "Fuck, Lily, you feel so good. Are you always this wet?"

I close my eyes, swallowing hard and concentrating on the magic of his caress and the way it incrementally transforms me into a being of unadulterated lust. "Only when I think of you," I confess, breathing hard.

"Oh yeah?" Surprise and seduction color his voice. He circles his left hand's cream-slick thumb around my clit while the fingers of his right penetrate and please me until I tremble beneath his touch. "And do you think of me often?"

"All the time," I pant as his finger finds the rough spot at the front of my pussy. "Yes, baby, that's it," I encourage.

"And do you touch yourself like this when you think about me?" he asks, his voice low and dangerous, and his cock pressed tightly into my back.

"I do," I reply. "But you touching me is way better."

"I'm glad you like it," he says, his fingers artfully moving in and out of me and amplifying my need. "You know, this could be just the beginning if you want it to be."

"I want it to be." The words topple out of my mouth between sharp breaths.

My pussy grips his finger, and his breath comes sporadically as he changes the angle of his stroke. "That's it, Strawberry. I want you to come for me." He tickles and teases my G-spot until I can't take it anymore. Burying my head in the pillow to silence my screams, I drench his hand.

"Fuck," he says through gritted teeth. "A man could get used to this."

I work hard to pant quietly next to him, feeling perfectly sated. But with Turner, it's not enough. I want more—all of him. "I need your cock."

His body stiffens behind me again, and he says, "Not like this. Not our first time. I want to spend hours pleasing you and driving you wild. I want you to beg for my cock."

I'm ready to beg now. "What's stopping you?" I ask quietly, shifting to look into his dreamy blue eyes. "This is our honeymoon, after all."

"I've made plans for you today with my sisters."

"Plans with your sisters? Wait, you've only ever talked about foster brothers."

"Their wives and girlfriends," he corrects. "You're going to love them, and they're going to love you. But not half as much as..." His voice trails off.

"As?" I ask breathlessly.

"Shit, I'm tired," he says, wrapping his arms and legs back around me and holding me tightly. "You feel so good in my arms." The last statement sounds dark, conflicted.

"You can't leave me wanting you like this and expect me to hang out with your sisters..."

He sticks his head up, checking the alarm clock on the bedstead. "Shit, we overslept. It's nearly nine-thirty."

"Nine-thirty? I'm surprised the kids aren't up."

"Actually, I think they are," he says, stretching beside me and nodding towards the window outside. As I strain my ears, I hear the faint giggles of children and Trix barking. But my eyes remain glued to Turner's handsome planes and the way his large cock tents in his pants.

"Thirsty, girl?" he asks with a handsome smile.

My cheeks burn, and I grumble, "I wish I didn't blush all the time. It's very annoying."

"I think it's adorable, actually," he replies. "My sisters will be here in about an hour, so it's time for you to get ready. After all, an hour's not nearly enough time for what I want to do to you." He says the last sentence like he's trying to convince himself.

"Why would you plan something with your sisters so early the day after our wedding?"

His face looks torn as if he's asking himself the same question. After a long pause, he replies, "I thought a fake wedding meant a fake honeymoon. But maybe I was wrong." Desire is written all over his face as he continues, "Now, if you'll excuse me, I've got a date with a cold shower because I can't take any more of seeing you like this...all sexy and satisfied by your husband."

I love the sound of that two-syllable word on his lips. He leans in, kissing me tenderly before jumping out of bed. Glancing back over his shoulder at me, he adds, "By the way, you're the most beautiful thing I've ever woken up next to." The emotion in his voice and eyes is undeniable as he drinks me in for one long moment before striding into the bathroom and closing the door.

Chapter Eighteen

LILY

The sight of Turner in nothing but a towel with wet hair and soft, freshly-shaven cheeks stops me in my tracks. But he's a man on a mission.

"Quit tempting me, woman," he orders. "My sisters will be here in thirty minutes, and I've got breakfast to make for the kids. If you hurry, you can get some coffee and French toast, too."

His voice has a teasing edge, and he smacks my ass playfully as I pass by him, headed for the shower. I've never seen the grumpy cowboy look happier, although I have trouble wrapping my head around the fact it has something to do with me.

He calls after me, "There are a few things we need to hash out before I head downstairs."

I turn, trying to keep my eyes on his face. "Yes?"

"How did we meet?" he asks. "You know, for my sisters..."

"How we really met," I say quietly. "At my parents' funeral."

His face tightens. "Wow, I didn't think you'd remember that. The whole town turned out, after all."

"You may be many things, Turner West, but forgettable isn't one of them."

He swallows hard. "And how did we fall in love?" He raises his eyebrow, flashing me a lopsided grin.

"You tell me," I reply, flirtatiously.

"Slowly, incrementally, and then all at once. You know, kind of like how inspiration hits an artist."

I smile, wondering what he knows about creative inspiration.

Nodding towards the bed, he observes, "You took the right side last night. Any particular reason?"

"Because it's furthest from the slider to the balcony...so you can keep me safe from any intruders or bears that try to sneak in the house."

He clears his throat, his cheeks darkening. "I'll never let anything hurt you, if it's up to me... Alright, enough chit-chat. You better hurry because they'll be here soon."

I shower quickly, my mind still enveloped in thoughts of my stunning husband and his very skilled hands. If he can do that to me with his fingers and thumb, I wonder what the rest of his well-endowed body is capable of.

After the shower, I put my luggage on the bed, shuffling through it to find the perfect outfit for a day out with Turner's sisters. I'd be lying if I said I wasn't scared. I know the "sister test" is one of the hardest to pass when merging families.

I want to make the best impression on them, even though I have no clue what's going on between my neighbor and me. All I know is we're both shitty at this whole fake marriage thing.

I'd be an idiot if I thought a round of finger-banging equated with lifelong commitment. Maybe he couldn't help himself... But I have trouble believing that, considering the self-control he showed in meeting my needs while denying his own.

I stare down at the modest diamond ring on my hand. I suppose any other girl would expect a fancy replacement from their millionaire husband. But there's something perfect about it and its sentimental value.

I know enough about Turner to realize he loved his mother dearly despite her problems. Gifting me this memento speaks volumes more than an expensive ring ever could.

Emotion knots tightly in my throat as I consider my return gift to him. He may not realize this, but putting my father's ring on his finger says everything about how much I esteem him.

It also speaks to the kind of man he is. There's no one else on this planet I would let wear that silly old band, even though I'd be lucky to pawn it for fifty dollars.

A soft knock sounds on the door as I stand in the mirror, taking one last look at the long, flowing navy blue dress I wear covered in large, pale roses. I've paired it with a jean jacket, a mint-colored scarf, and a cute pair of dark brown ankle boots.

"Sissy," Poppy's voice says, and I turn, welcoming her into my open arms. "You look pretty."

"Hi, sweetie," I whisper, stroking her hair. "Did you sleep okay?"

She nods as I examine her bright cheeks and open expression.

She observes, "You look tired, sis." This sentence has me second-guessing my decision not to wear makeup.

"I am. I had a little trouble sleeping last night. Do you think I could use a little makeup?"

Her wide blue eyes scrutinize me before she nods.

"Turner wanted me to come and get you," she whispers. "His sisters are here."

"Oh shoot. Follow me into the bathroom while I finish

getting ready." I grab my emerald green makeup bag, and we head into Turner's palatial white bathroom.

Poppy whispers, "Lily, why did you marry the neighbor? You barely know him."

Her words alarm me. Not only is she speaking the truth, but if she said any part of this to Darlene from CPS, it would be the end of our entire ruse. Shaking my head and working hard to clear groggy cobwebs from my brain, I reply, "You're too young to understand."

She eyes me curiously, saying, "I don't get it. He's almost as old as Daddy." Her face starts to shatter at the word "Daddy," and I cup her cheek, stroking it gently and speaking calming words.

"He's much younger than Dad, although I know he acts grumpy and old sometimes. But he's a good man. One of the best, as far as I can tell, and he's helping to keep our family together. Besides, he's handsome, polite, and safe. He's all of those things."

She scrunches her face, confused.

Looking into the mirror, I apply some blush to brighten my cheeks and a dash of mascara to my red-hued eyelashes to provide more contrast. A little pale lip gloss, and I've covered my exhaustion the best I can.

"You'll understand as you get older. Not everything's like a fairy tale. Especially when it comes to love. Now, why don't you tell Turner I'll be right down."

As I watch her reflection in the mirror skip away, I realize I just used the four-letter word "love" to describe what's happening between Turner and me. There's no more fitting word, even though it terrifies me.

Don't get ahead of yourself, Lily. Your marriage is fake. But I can't help myself. Not only do I want to get ahead of myself. I want to time travel to tonight and the delicious pleasures awaiting me when I see my handsome cowboy again.

I hurry downstairs to the sound of female voices in the entryway. Cinnamon, vanilla, and maple syrup waft from the kitchen. Turner wears a dark green half-apron, and stands at the door, hugging four beautiful plus-sized twenty-some-things. They could be my sisters...*if they had the telltale Monroe red hair.*

One has a curly mane of black hair and crystal blue eyes. As I approach, Turner wraps his arm possessively around my waist, introducing, "Lily, this is my sister-in-law, Alex. She's married to my brother, Maksim." I take her soft hand, nodding, and she does the same with a reserved grin.

Next to her is a stylish blonde dressed to the nines. Her face is serious, and she scrutinizes me curiously. She doesn't wait for Turner to say anything. Instead, she leans forward, assertively offering her hand, "I'm Jess, and I'm married to Logan." My head is already swimming. I don't know how I'll keep everyone's name straight.

But then it hits me. "You mean Logan Caples?"

She nods, her face beaming.

He's a tall, talkative, black-haired and black-bearded search and rescue guy. "He comes into the Silver Fork with all the search and rescue people for breakfast. He tips well."

Jess nods. "And I bet he and Louis talk your ear off."

I laugh. "Yes, they do."

Turner's face tightens, and I swear he looks jealous. Guiding me down the line further, he says, "This is Faith, and she's married to my brother, Travis."

Faith has light brown hair with blonde streaks and large brown eyes that look open and friendly. Instead of taking my hand, she leans in to hug me, saying, "I know you."

I serve her and her hunky firefighter husband, Travis, often at the Silver Fork. They couldn't be more in love, and their baby, Ryder, is adorable.

Faith continues, "We're so happy to welcome you into the

family. You couldn't do better than Turner. He's my favorite brother, apart from Travis, of course."

"You know I'm telling Logan that," Jess teases.

Alex chimes in, "Maksim won't care as long as people leave him alone. He's more of a dog person than a people person."

"Except with you," Jess teases, wrapping her arm around Alex's waist. They look comfortable together...as if they've known each other their whole lives.

"Well, I should be your favorite brother, too," Turner chimes in, looking at Alex. "Seeing as we're finally expanding your cabin this summer."

The black-haired woman with piercing eyes claps her hands together excitedly. "We can't wait to have more room... and privacy."

Turner nods. "You two better think long and hard about how many more rooms you want to add. My guess is you're in for a big family—something I thought I'd never say in the context of my antisocial baby brother."

She pipes in, "He's perfectly social with me..." The whole group laughs, and her cheeks darken as she realizes what she said.

"That's exactly my point, Alex. So, maybe think about an additional room or two."

At the end of the line, I see Jasmine, the curvy raven-haired Latina girl with a round face and full red lips, who always comes in with her boss and boyfriend, Flynn.

"Lily!" she exclaims, hugging me. I love the beautiful Spanish lilt to her accent. "I was so excited and surprised to hear about you and Turner."

After a few minutes of small talk, Jess says, "Alright, bro, we're stealing your girl to get the lowdown on everything you've obviously been keeping from us. The men-folk will be over shortly to help out. They had to go to the ranch this morning. I'm not sure how you got out of it."

"Pops gave me a break, considering I'm a newly married man. But I'm sure I'll catch shit for it later. Have fun, you girls. Lily will be right out. I need to have a quick word with her."

With his arm still around my waist, he nudges me towards the living room as Rosie and Jack run past, screaming at the top of their lungs.

"Walking feet," I chide as Turner's eyes shoot daggers their way. How in the world is he going to handle all five of them without me today? Is that what his sisters meant by the men helping out?

"Are you sure you want me to leave you with all the kids?"

"I'll manage," he says, frowning as Cole sprints by with Trix at his heels. "Outside, everyone," he hollers before turning back to me. "Give me your phone, Lily," he demands.

"Why?"

"Because you should have my number. Don't hesitate to call me if you need anything." I watch him program his number into my phone, a strange, unexplained warmth radiating through me. Outside of my dad, I've never had a man I could call or count on before. It's a strange and wonderful feeling.

Reaching into his back pocket, he fishes out a wad of one-hundred-dollar bills, handing them to me. I don't count it, but I'm guessing there's at least a thousand dollars in the bundle. "If you need more, let me know."

I'm stunned into silence, unable to think. The way he throws around money is unbelievable. Especially since I white knuckle every nickel and dime that comes my way. "W-why are you giving this to me?"

He levels his gaze on me, and my breath catches in my throat as I take in his stunning, stormy eyes. "Because no wife of mine would want for anything." He looks away, and I swear his cheeks are a shade darker.

Returning his gaze to mine with a newfound intensity that nearly knocks me flat, he warns, "Jess is a true crime reporter who works for the *Chronicle*, and she's got a bullshit meter like none other. So, you'll have to come up with something you like about me when she asks. And it's got to be believable. Because I know her, and a thousand questions are brewing in her head."

His words stun me. It would be easier to come up with a list of what I don't like about him. *Does he not realize this?* Instead, I say drily, "In other words, don't fuck this up."

He cracks an involuntary smile, his brows still knitted together. His face looks disturbed, no doubt by the chaos of small children stampeding through his impeccably decorated home. "That's right. Don't fuck it up."

I nod, too caught up in his gorgeous eyes to think straight. Taking my cheeks in his palms, he leans down. His soft, warm lips feather over mine, nipping my lips and dancing lightly and tenderly over them, teasing me with the tip of his tongue. Heat surges through my core as his mouth sparks over mine, igniting every bit of flesh he touches on fire, the most delicious fire I've ever felt, until I lean into him, desperate for more.

My heart dances in my chest, and I exhale as he presses back into me, deepening the kiss until I feel tremors in my toes. My lips part, and his tongue sinks into my mouth, claiming me with a masculine authority I've never experienced before. It fills my veins and arteries with fire.

I can't help myself. My arms snake around his neck, and I let out a soft moan as the stroke of his kiss turns suggestive. His hands drop from my cheeks to my hips, squeezing my waist and drawing me hard against his arousal.

I gasp, melting into him as desire rocks my whole body, knocking the wind from my lungs. My chest feels like a hummingbird has taken up residence. I tighten my grip on his neck, pulling him into me with enthusiastic abandon.

"Ew!" Jack screams behind us, accompanied by the pitter-patter of small feet on wood floors, and Rosie chimes in, "And they lived happily ever after."

Turner's hands leave my waist, and he steps back, scolding, "Outside. I already told you. Everyone outside, and that means Trix, too." His face looks frustrated and flustered as he turns back to me, running his hand through his hair and frowning grimly. "If you can't think of anything else you like about me, maybe tell Jess and the other girls that I'm a halfway decent kisser."

His lopsided grin steals my heart.

"More than halfway," I mutter quietly, and his face looks vindicated.

"Alright, go have fun on your girls' day out. Just remember what you say so you can fill me in over a warm glass of milk tonight. You know so that we can keep our stories straight." He winks, turning and striding towards the sliding door in the kitchen.

Stopping suddenly, he looks back over his shoulder, adding, "Oh, and make sure you get up earlier in the future. Rumor has it my brunches are pretty damn good...even for an uneducated country bumpkin. Although they won't hold a candle to your fancy French pastries. But as I promised last night, I'm working on that with Cricket."

I open my mouth to remind him he's the reason I'm up so late. But a loud crash sounds next to us, startling me into silence.

Turner orders, "Get your asses... I mean, butts outside now!" Cole and Trix freeze. Amid roughhousing, they've knocked one of his metal sculptures over. I can only imagine how much it's worth.

"I'm so sorry—" I start.

But he cuts me off, shaking his head. "You better get out of here before I change my mind about watching these...kids."

His face is rigid, and his eyes narrow as I stand immovable, torn about leaving him alone with my siblings. This is a recipe for disaster. He adds, "Remember you're doing this for your brothers and sisters."

"And why are you doing this?" I ask breathlessly. I know what he's already told me, but there has to be more. Right? Especially after this morning.

"I already told you. To right a past wrong." He looks like he has more to say, but instead, he presses his gorgeous, kiss-able lips firmly together.

Chapter Nineteen

TURNER

osie, Jack, and Cole run around wildly, playing tag with each other and Trix. I can't figure out what rules they're following or even who's "it," but a deep rumble of laughter fills my chest as I watch their antics.

Everything about the last twenty-four hours is surreal. But I can't focus on that now because I have far too much on my mind.

My brothers will be here within the hour to help me start repairing the Monroe place. So much work needs to be done. And there's no telling when we'll finish. But I can't think of a better time to dive into this project, seeing as warmer weather will usher in my busy season.

A deep ache fills my chest at the thought of Lily ever leaving me. It's completely irrational. Simultaneously, the thought of another late-night rendezvous over warm mugs of milk has my stomach in knots and my pulse in overdrive.

Can my feelings get anymore jumbled? My mind wanders to the potential after-party, and my breath catches. Yes, they can.

Cole runs up to me, holding a frisbee he found in the

backyard. He sure is good at finding what's not his. 'Thanks, buddy," I say, ruffling his crimson hair. "Let's see how Trix does fetching this."

I launch the plastic missile in the air, and Trix chases after it like a silver cheetah, pure muscle and speed. Jumping high into the air, he catches it at the height of the disc's upward trajectory, and Cole lets out a "Whoop!" It reminds me of a documentary I once saw of a caracal hunting birds.

"Did you see that?" The troublemaker asks, his voice filled with awe.

"Shit, yeah." I swallow hard at the stricken look on the boy's face. "I mean, hell yeah." Nope, still not kid-friendly enough. "I mean, yeah."

Cole cocks his head to the side. "You're not used to being around kids much. Are you, mister?"

I shake my head. "Sometimes, I feel like I'm babysitting all day long at work if that counts?"

The kid squints his eyes as if a closer examination of me will clarify what I'm saying. He's far too young to appreciate my sarcasm.

"You want to throw it this time?"

He kicks the ground, shaking his head. "Nope," he grumbles.

"What's the matter, kid?"

He stares at me long and hard. Finally, he asks, "You promise you won't tell anyone?"

I nod.

"I'm no good at throwing a frisbee. Everyone makes fun of me at school when I try."

Trix and Cole both look expectantly at me, wide-eyed and waiting. "I can show you how to throw a frisbee. It's all in the wrist."

More than fifty throws later, the boy's arm doesn't look half bad. He squeals in delight as he throws his longest frisbee launch yet, making it to my property's tree line as Trix barrels behind it. I high-five Cole, and his eyes fill with wonder as he looks up at me. Like I'm a fucking superhero or something. It makes me puff out my chest with pride. *Is this what it feels like to be a dad?*

"I can't believe you taught me how to do that!"

I shrug. "You did it all yourself, kid. You've got a good throwing arm. There's plenty else I could teach you, too. Like how to pitch a baseball and how to grip and release a football. Do you play any sports?"

"I used to play Little League. But Lily says we won't have enough money for it in the spring." He looks down, his face scrunching.

The kitchen slider whirs behind me, and I hear Poppy's voice call across the yard. "And I used to play softball. I was getting pretty good...until, you know." Her voice trails off sadly.

Daisy stands next to her, nodding her head. "Me, too."

The main thing I remember about the Monroes is them always driving somewhere. Now, I understand why. Thankfully, none of the children were with Donovan and Vera when the fatal accident occurred.

The three older kids' sorrow feels palpable, even as Jack and Rosie tear around in the distance, chasing each other and giggling until their faces are the same shade as their hair.

"I lost my mom when I was young, too," I say quietly. "Can't imagine losing both parents, though. Life isn't fair. Not one bit."

"No, it isn't," Poppy replies, exhaling slowly and blinking hard not to cry.

Daisy puts her head in her hands, and Poppy wraps her arm around her, comforting her quietly.

"Lily's had it hard caring for you all by herself. I want to make things easier on her and all of you."

Poppy's eyes snap to my face. "Is that why you married her?"

Her penetrating gaze surprises me, and there's a wordiness and wisdom to her that only comes from great suffering far too young. I know the look well.

I nod, searching hard for the right words. "Yep, I want to make her life better and care for her. Care for all of you, too. Sometimes in life, you get a chance to right a wrong. Maybe you can't go back and change the past, but you can fix the future. Does that make sense?"

Poppy knits her brows together, deep in thought, and I can see her mind churning over what to say.

Before she can get out her next thought, Daisy cuts her off, asking, "I thought people only got married when they love each other. But you barely know my sister. Are you going to treat her right?"

The girl's precocious words put a cold sweat on my forehead. I feel like I'm getting interrogated by the FBI or something. And the concern radiating from their eyes in my direction makes me feel like I've got a spotlight on my face.

"Sometimes it takes a long time for people to fall in love. That's usual, really. But other times, you just know the first moment you set eyes on them. You may not understand the how or the why of it, and you may fight it with every ounce of your being, but it's inevitable. And one day, if you're not too pigheaded, you finally give into your feelings and accept the gift God has given you."

Poppy and Daisy's faces melt at the words, and they smile.

But Cole's having none of my ambiguous answer. "Do you love my sister or not? It's a 'yes' or 'no' question."

I stare at the boy, really thinking through his query. After all, I know I'm about to get the fifth degree from my brothers. So, I better come up with something good to say.

I want to protect her and keep her safe. I want to provide for her and ensure she never has to work a day in her life...unless she wants to. I want to see her smile more, and maybe just once, smile solely for me.

I rub the spot on my chest where a dull ache has inexplicably nestled since the pretty redhead left the house this morning. I don't know why it's there, and I'd rather not think about it. But the intensity of it keeps growing each time I see Lily... Despite the fact I'm not her type, and she isn't exactly mine.

I can't say any of the shit I'm thinking. But I do have to say something, so I go with a truth that should keep them thinking for a while. "My heart feels better when she's around. That's it. And, obviously, I want to keep your family together—"

"And become a part of our family, too, right?" Poppy asks.

What's up with these kids and the difficult questions? I shrug. "I guess so."

Cole looks skeptical. Taking a deep breath, he says, "I don't know. You've been pretty grumpy to me in the past."

"Yeah, because you're a little thief that keeps getting into my workshop," I snap back before I catch myself.

Poppy and Daisy's eyebrows jump into their hairlines, and Cole nods. "See, I told you both. He's grumpier than you think."

"Don't expect me to be nice when you're stealing my tools and gloves," I warn gruffly.

Cole crosses his arms, looking me boldly in the face, "Mister, I've told you once, and I'll tell you again. I've never stealed nothing from you."

"Stolen anything," I correct reflexively. I can tell by his puzzled expression, he doesn't get it. "Don't make things worse by lying—"

The percussive sound of wheels on gravel interrupts me mid-thought. I hand the frisbee to Cole, matching his glare with my own. There may be a lot I'll put up with from this rambunctious group because of their gorgeous older sister. But stealing and thieving aren't among them. Leveling my gaze on Poppy, I order, "My brothers are here. Keep an eye on your siblings while I go let them in."

Stomping through the house, I survey the daily chaos already caused. A metal statue needs to be welded back together, and dirty paw prints discolor my white couch.

"Motherfucker," I grumble under my breath. Kids and dogs are vortices of destruction. Why the fuck does my pretty little Strawberry have to come with both of them?

She's not your "pretty little Strawberry," Turner. Fuck, I'm losing my grip. Despite the sexy morning delight, I can't assume there's anything more between Lily and me. Although heaven knows I'd like there to be.

At the front door, a line of curious eyes greet me. I can tell by the looks on their faces that my brothers have a million questions, and by the impatient way they breeze past me into the house, grabbing stools and chairs to sit on, they're ready for a rapid-fire Spanish Inquisition.

I grab a chair, sitting down as my brothers circle me, managing to put me in the center. I frown, ready for their shit, even as I keep a watchful eye on the kids outside.

Flynn starts. The ebony-skinned cowboy lawyer is known for his poker face, and I find it eerie that I still have trouble reading his expression after so many years as brothers.

"The prenup looks good, and your marriage documents are in order. And I see you've got an insta-family outside, which I know a little about. But what the fuck, man? Weren't you telling me the other day how you do everything to avoid Lily Monroe because she's too young for you?"

His question may be longer and more complicated than the children's, but the theme remains the same. *Do I or don't I love Lily?*

I know what logic and reason tell me. We barely know

each other. It's too soon. She married me for my money and home. I'm not even her type.

But my heart says something very different. The same thing it's been saying for three months. That the girl of my dreams...my soulmate, is right in front of me. If I'm too scared to do anything about it, though, I could lose her before ever making her mine.

As I bobble my head back and forth between Flynn and my other brothers, Logan, Maksim, and Travis, a weird tranquility comes over me. Shaking my head, I realize I don't have to have all of the answers. I just have to listen to my heart.

"I can't answer that. All I know is the thought of living without her seriously fucks with my head."

Logan, the search and rescue lead, nods, saying, "I remember when my head started twisting that way for Jess. I never in a million years thought that blonde would be my undoing. Now, she's my everything."

Because of Lily, I now understand Logan's words. I get how an inveterate player and ladies' man can change overnight for the right woman.

Travis and Maksim, my younger brothers, have far less to say, but I can tell they get where I'm coming from. "I know I called you guys over here to help with repairs at the Monroe place. But there's something I need your help with even more."

"Anything," Travis pipes up.

"In that case, let's head out to my workshop," I order. "You're going to need your welding gear."

Chapter Twenty

"Some country music I can get behind," Jess says, taking another bite of the bacon she fished out of her BLT a moment ago. "Like that song 'I Had Some Help' by Post Malone. That's an okay number."

"Yeah, it's alright," Faith counters. "But I like romantic music like Faith Hill, Luke Combs, and George Strait."

"Dated!" Jess retorts.

Looking at me, Faith asks, "You like country music, right, Lily? I can't imagine you don't since you married our brother."

I shrug. Thankfully, I know a little something about this subject, thanks to Turner's musical selection while in his workshop. "He also likes classic and modern rock, so we have plenty in common."

Faith nods, looking a little disappointed.

Jess butts in. "Here's my final word on the subject. Country's alright... Thankfully, it's not a prerequisite to enjoying life in Rough & Ready Country."

Her last statement piques my curiosity. "Are you originally from around here?"

Her eyebrows shoot up. "Oh, Turner hasn't told you?"

I freeze, kicking myself for the stupid question, even though it's far from stupid to me. I shake my head, looking down.

"So, Alex and I grew up in San Francisco together. We were next-door neighbors. Alex is a famous classical cellist, although she'll never admit it. And I write true crime for the *Chronicle*."

I'm stunned that two highly successful, big-city women have chosen to make their home here. "Do you like living in Rough & Ready?" I ask curiously.

Both nod emphatically, and I can tell they're not faking their answers. I shake my head. "What do you like about being here?"

Jess, the fast-paced and assertive talker in the group, replies, "I've honestly never seen more beautiful country in my entire life. Logan has taken me to private places on the ranch that few human eyes have ever seen."

"I'm sure he has," Faith teases, reaching across the table to pinch Jess.

"Well, that's another subject," the pretty blonde journalist quips with an unrepentant nod.

Jasmine chimes in, "So, my family's from SoCal. They own a big ranch outside of Temecula, and it's a gorgeous location. But I agree, there's something about this cowboy country that gets in your blood and won't let go. Turner told me you're a very talented artist, so I'm sure it'll prove doubly true for you."

"He did?" I ask, surprised. "What else did he say about me?"

Alex's brow knits together, and she adds, "It's not so much what he says but how he acts around you. I've never seen him look at another woman the way he looks at you. I'm not sure what you did, but the man worships the ground you walk on."

My cheeks burn, and I know they've turned some ungodly shade of red. Transparent emotions will always be my torch to bear. I think back to what Turner said this morning, that he thought my blushing was adorable, and desire lodges in my throat.

As much fun as I'm having with the girls at the Silver Fork for lunch, I can't wait to get home to my handsome cowboy. It scares me because the man could break my heart. And even though everything about this morning felt beyond amazing, all I know for sure is our marriage is fake. Despite the risks, though, the anticipation of seeing him tonight has me floating on clouds of joy.

Somehow, over the past three months, my feelings for Turner have snuck up on me. Everytime I admired his incredible physique and soulful eyes. Everytime I argued with him, fighting with every cell in my body not to acknowledge the truth. Everytime I caught him staring awkwardly at me in return. Not only am I seeing the last three months in a totally different light, but I'm finally allowing myself to admit what my heart has always known.

"So, what do you like about him?" Faith questions enthusiastically.

I open my mouth, but Jess cuts me off. "By the way, whatever you do, don't ask Faith what she likes about Travis. That woman could write a dissertation about my heartthrob brother."

Faith snickers, nodding. "That's what happens when you get to marry your dreamy best friend."

What do I like about Turner? Didn't he ask me something similar last night, only I lied, saying he wasn't my type?

I lick my lips, working hard to transform the overwhelming flood of emotions, impressions, and memories into something coherent. "I'll spare you guys what I think about him looks-wise because we all know he's gorgeous."

The women staring curiously at me look pleased by my assessment.

"But beyond good looks, he's incredibly generous, decisive, and a real problem solver. He makes me feel safe and lets me put my guard down so that I can quit worrying about *everything*...you know, the way I was before the accident."

My voice cracks, and I stop for a long moment, biting my lower lip and breathing slowly to stop myself from crying. Today's supposed to be fun, not a cry-fest. "He's smart, witty, and a real feeling man. He may not admit it, but I can tell he has soulful thoughts and loves hard. Really hard. And he might not admit this, either, but he has the qualities to be a good dad."

I finish, looking up and half smiling. Faith has tears in her eyes, and Jess and Alex's faces beam. To my surprise, Jasmine's eyes well, too, and she says, "Thank goodness you found each other. You're exactly what he needs."

Alex explains, "Unlike the other brothers, Turner is more talkative when it comes to women. He's confided a lot in us girls, and we want desperately to see him happy."

Jess nods in agreement. "It's always been hard for Turner, I think, compared to the rest of the brothers because he's such a naturally artsy guy..."

Artsy? What does she mean? Like with the homes he builds?

"...And yes, he feels things more deeply than he's willing to admit. I think that's why he's avoided a long-term commitment up to this point. Because he doesn't want to get his heart broken or lose someone he loves again... You know about his mom, right?"

Do I? I can't honestly answer this question. I know a bit

about his mother. But Jess's question makes me feel like there's a lot more. That said, I know what Turner's real fiancée would say. "I do," I reply quietly, putting my hand on the table. "This is her ring."

"Shit, that's romantic," Jess exclaims, her jaw dropping. "I know that's not a ton of karats or probably worth much. But I hope you understand the significance of him giving that ring to you."

I nod confidently, and all eyes are on me. "Because I gave him my dad's wedding band in return..." My voice trails off as I fight to keep it together. *Will it ever get easier to talk about my parents?* "I know it's not worth much, and I half thought he wouldn't want to wear it...you know, with what happened. But he didn't even hesitate. He's the only man on the planet I would let wear that ring."

Jasmine fans her face to fight more tears, and Faith unabashedly wipes her eyes with her napkin. Alex uses the back of her hand, and Jess blinks back moisture.

"Okay, we need a change of subject right now, or else I'm going to be sobbing in a moment," the blonde says, shaking her head. She raises her hands in the air. "All I can say is between your creativeness and sentimentality, you two are cut from the same cloth. I'm so glad you found each other!"

I push my Cobb salad around on the plate, stirring the blue cheese dressing and bacon into the lettuce leaves. I'm unsure what else to say. I still feel overwhelmed, trying to get to know so many amazing women in one go. But something nags at the back of my mind.

"Turner kept telling me I was way too young for him. But I know Flynn's older than you by a fair amount, Jasmine, and the same has to be true for you and Logan, Jess. Do you have any issues because of the age difference?"

Jasmine laughs. "Yeah, I remember Flynn using that as a

reason we couldn't get together. Well, that and the fact I was his employee. But it was an excuse because he thought I wasn't into him. I was in an on-again, off-again relationship when I started working for him, which was a whole thing."

Jess nods, listening attentively. She adds, "Logan was a little freaked out because I'm eleven years younger than him. But honestly, it doesn't matter from day to day now that we're together. And I find his maturity and masculinity hotter than hell. I could never go back to dating baby boys my age."

"Yeah, I was never into older guys. But with Turner, I definitely see the allure... And no, I'd never want to go back to guys my own age again."

"It's like that Hey Violet song," Jess notes, singing the chorus. "And just so you know, I'd take his concerns with a grain of salt. The guy's been crushing hard on you ever since you came to town. Ask any one of us." She looks around the table, and every head nods. "We've all had to hear about you and his excuses for keeping you at arm's length. I'm glad he finally gave up trying."

"Me, too," I reply with an ear-to-ear grin. My heart pounds. As much as I'm enjoying the girls' company, every part of me longs to be back in the arms of my mountain man.

Roxanne has served us throughout our lunch, and she approaches the table, asking, "To-go boxes?" She counts the show of hands and returns five minutes later with five boxes.

We've been talking for hours, and I look down at my cell phone, seeing it's two thirty. No wonder the Silver Fork has suddenly gone dead. The lunch rush is over.

Flipping up the many notifications, I notice a text from "Husband," realizing that's how Turner typed his contact information in my phone. I swallow hard, feeling warm and gooey inside. God, I need him so badly right now. I cross my legs hard, trying to put the kibosh on my insistent yearning for him.

I unlock my phone and read:

"How are you doing, Strawberry?"

An instant smile captures my face, and Jess teases, "Looks like somebody got a text from their man."

This makes Turner's sisters pull out their phones. Soon, grins light up around the table.

I type back:

"I can't stop thinking about this morning."

A moment later, I get:

"Neither can I, and I can't wait to see you again."

Blood surges through my veins as a wistful sigh escapes me. I reply:

"Neither can I."

I punctuate it with the lips emoji, locking my screen and fanning myself. Faith's doing the same. Our eyes lock, and we both start laughing. She explains, "I've got a good texter, too."

"Logan's terrible at texting," Jess responds. "But I like the pictures he sends."

"Ew," Alex exclaims. "TMI!"

Jasmine adds, "Seriously, I could have lived a lifetime without knowing that."

We all stand up from the booth to the sounds of squeaking vinyl, pausing for a moment to check that we have our purses, phones, and takeout boxes.

"Where to next?" I ask, trying to sound cheerful, even though every part of me longs to be at Turner's cabin with him.

"Ophir City, where the good shopping is," Jasmine answers.

I feel a firm hand on my arm, and Roxanne says, "Hey, Lily, can I talk to you alone for a moment?"

I call after the girls. "I'll be out in a minute. I want to talk to Roxy." They nod and continue walking to the door as I follow the black-haired waitress back through the kitchen. I wave to Jerry as we pass, and he screams, "We're gonna miss you, Lil!"

I nod, smiling, and head out to the scuzzy lot where I learned about my burned house yesterday. What has transpired in little more than twenty-four hours remains impossible to quantify.

In muted tones, Roxanne says, "I heard about your marriage, and I feel terrible I didn't tell you this sooner..." The way her voice trails off, and she looks away, worries me.

"What is it?" I ask breathlessly.

"Remember Thursday morning when you had me switch tables with you because you didn't want to serve Turner and that older guy, Broderick?"

I nod, my heart racing.

"Well, I overheard them talking. Turner was trying to get Broderick to give him his company after retirement. And Broderick wasn't into it because he said Turner was scared of settling down and getting married. He said he wanted his company to go to a man who knew how to commit."

"What are you saying?" I ask, my mouth going dry and my stomach falling.

"The old guy told Turner he had to get married to take over the company. I can't get that conversation out of my mind. And then I started thinking about how Turner's brother is the sheriff and has ties to CPS. And I hate to say this, but what if he came up with this whole child custody thing to make you marry him?"

I cover my mouth with my hand as her words coil around my mind. Although she was a great coworker, my thoughts settle on the way I saw her flirting with Turner. I shake my head. "I just can't believe he'd be manipulative like that."

She narrows her eyes, scrutinizing me. *Or would he?*

From past conversations, I know she's lived on the reservation on the outskirts of town her whole life. Although she's too young to have gone to school with Turner, she has to know him far better than I do.

Roxy continues, "But it makes sense. And it's pretty obvious he was never into you until the whole marriage thing came up with his boss. Even the day I served him, he never looked your direction once."

I shake my head vigorously now. But my assessment of him Thursday morning was very similar to Roxy's. "There's no way. His sisters just got done going on and on about how Turner has been crushing on me for months. He tried to hide his feelings because of my age. But no, I can't believe what you're saying."

Skepticism storms in her face.

"And Christian said the same thing, that Turner's liked me ever since I came to Rough & Ready," I add.

"And what do they all have in common? They're family, sweetie. And I think you've figured out by now, a very tight-knit family. So, can you trust any of them?"

I don't know what to say. Instead, I press my lips firmly together. Everything about her narrative feels wrong, but I'd be lying if I said it didn't play on my deepest insecurities.

Roxy argues, "No offense, but you're definitely not his type. I've known Turner for years, and he's always into those skinny Minnie types who spend their days at the gym."

My ears ring, and my stomach aches acutely like I've been sucker-punched. The conversation with Turner's sisters lingers in my mind. But Roxy's narrative makes sense, especially in the context of my dating history. Men have always used me. I squeeze my eyes tightly, trying not to freak out.

Then, a revelation hits me hard...

This is why the handsome cowboy passed up sleeping with me this morning. No guy I've ever been with has had that kind of self-control... He's faking his attraction to me but couldn't bring himself to do the deed with me.

133

My face falls, and my hands fist at my sides.

Roxanne hugs me, saying, "I'm so sorry I had to tell you this, but I couldn't live with myself if I didn't. From one plus-sized gal to another, I think he's using you, Lily. Guys like that, you know millionaires, only want girls like us for one reason. And it's never long-term."

Chapter Twenty-One

TURNER

What a fucking day! My head still reels as I replay everything that happened. My brothers and I got next to nothing done on the Monroe place. But it'll have to wait because I had a far more pressing matter that needed our attention.

I hope Lily will appreciate it. All I know is after this morning, I haven't been able to think straight. And every cell in my body yearns to answer the question she had last night—about why I make my house, no, my home, in Rough & Ready Country.

Maybe I'm a fucking fool, though. How in the world could I ever compare to a place like Paris? Thinking about how her face lights up when she talks about that city makes me jealous. I've never been envious of a geographic location before. *How is that even a thing?*

But I must admit, there's not much I wouldn't give to see her talk about me with that kind of passion...*just once.*

I shake my head. I've lost my fucking mind.

My cellphone buzzes, and I flip up the screen. I have a text from Jess. I don't know whether to fear or welcome it.

"Bro, we're turning onto four eighty-eight now. Be there in fifteen... I don't know what you've done, but this girl's head over heels for you. She couldn't stop talking about you at lunch. Don't worry...all good stuff. Like gushingly, gross, kinda TMI good stuff."

An ear-to-ear grin captures my face, and my heart bangs against my ribs. I rub my hand over my face, taking deep breaths to calm my pulse. *Take it down a notch, Turner. After all, you did warn her she'd have to lay it on thick for Jess.*

But as the minutes tick by, I can't help myself. My cheeks flush, and I feel like I stuck a fork in an electrical outlet. I'm a fucking live wire from head to toe, and I can't wait to see my beautiful Strawberry again. *I've lost it. I've finally fucking lost it.*

Women always let you down, Turner. You can't trust them. Just look at your mom. A couple of years ago, this self-talk would've put me off Lily for good. Because honestly, I like her so much, it scares the shit out of me.

After seeing how happy all of my brothers are, though, I can't help but think there might be a girl God made just for me. And heck, if every part of my being isn't telling me Lily's the one.

The front door opens, and I hear a rustle of shopping bags as Lily's lovely voice calls out, "Thank you again, sisters! I had a total blast!"

I exhale sharply. *Sisters?* It must've gone well. The front door shuts to the sound of a car backing up on gravel, and I rush to the front door to help Lily with her bags. She's bent over, setting down her purchases, and I can't help but admire her lovely round ass and full hips. Fuck, the thought of squeezing those luscious hips as she rides me makes my cock jump.

She turns at the sound of my footsteps, straightening, and we both stare at each other, unmoving.

I lean forward to pull her into my arms for another kiss. But at that exact second, she turns, motioning towards the bags that need carrying. I stop short, running my hand through my hair and feeling instantly awkward.

Her voice squeaks as she says, "You really did wait up for warm milk."

I nod, my fucking mouth uncontrollably breaking into another grin. *Okay, what in the fuck is wrong with me?* I've always considered myself cool around the ladies, but for some damn reason, I feel like the geek at high school prom.

"I hope you won't be disappointed then," she says icily, and my heart sinks.

"You must be tired. Are you going straight to bed?" I ask, trying not to sound out of breath.

"Oh, no, I'm not tired at all. But I need a drink." Fishing through the bags and giving me another gorgeous view of her ass, she triumphantly pulls out a bottle of wine and a charcuterie plate. "Jasmine wanted to stop in at Napa-Sonoma. She and Flynn swear by this stuff."

"I could use a glass of wine," I reply, relieved she won't be retiring soon.

"Was it that rough with my siblings?" she asks, concern washing over her face. But there's a coldness in her voice that I can't place.

"How about I take your bags upstairs, and you break out the wine and snacks? I'd rather talk over booze."

"Me, too," she says nervously. "Promise me you won't look in the bags."

"I promise." Those two words barely leave my mouth before I kick myself for saying them. As I silently head towards the bedroom, my imagination races. Is there lingerie in the bags? Sexy panties? What the fuck doesn't she want me to see?

I know I'm jumping the gun, but I can't get my mind out

of the gutter. Setting the bags on the bed, I fight the urge to look. Fuck, it sucks being a man of my word sometimes.

I have to get my shit together because, for whatever reason, my expectations have gone through the roof between this morning and Jess's text.

But am I ready to alter my life permanently for a woman with five exhausting children and a menace of a dog? The answer knots my guts even tighter than the initial question.

Shit, I'm in trouble.

Lily has the bottle of wine open and two glasses out with generous pours of the ruby-colored liquid. The charcuterie plate sits in the middle, with two plates next to it.

"Let's eat in the living room at the coffee table," I suggest.

Her face freezes.

"What's wrong?"

"I don't want to risk spilling wine on your couch or anything."

I wave away her concern. "After you see what Trix and the kids did to it today... Well, let me just say, wine spills are the least of my concerns."

She covers her mouth with her hand, her eyebrow jumping to the top of her forehead. "I'm... I'm so sorry, Turner," she stammers.

I shrug. "You win some, and you lose some. At least all of the children are still alive and peacefully asleep."

"I know. How in the world did you manage the sleeping part?"

Shrugging, I say, "I grew up in a foster home. So, I know how to deal with kids. It's just that I don't usually have to."

Trix grumbles from his crate, annoyed by the noise we're making.

After we move everything to the coffee table, I find a couple of candles and light them, placing them next to the food. "This way, we can see what we're eating without upsetting his royal highness's sleep." I nod towards the Weimaraner in the crate.

Settling back into the couch cushions, I realize the candles are a terrible idea. The way the light reflects on Lily's stunning face has my jaw on the ground. My heart aches with an acuteness I've never felt before.

Lily swallows hard, returning my gaze until the heat and tension between us feel palpable. Neither of us moves. We just soak each other up with our eyes until I swear I'm looking straight into her agonizingly beautiful soul... But despite the intimate looks, her face is unreadable.

What the fuck is going on? And is it hitting her the same way it's hitting me? I wish I could tell.

I grab my glass of wine, breaking the moment. Otherwise, I'm about to do something stupid. Something very fucking stupid for a man who's fake married.

She follows suit, grabbing her glass and taking a sip. I lick my lips slowly, trying to memorize everything about her. How she looks with the candlelight warming her face, the smell of her strawberry-scented hair, the way her eyes drop to my lips, and they dilate.

"How was your day?" I ask gruffly, working hard to master the need rising in my core.

"Fine," she squeaks, taking another sip. "I'm surprised you're okay with me drinking. I thought for sure you'd try to card me or something." Her voice sounds testy.

Is she flirting with me or angry?

"I thought about it," I tease, transfixed by her ivory skin and thick pink lips. That fucking seam in her bottom lip will be the death of me. I long to trace it with my tongue before devouring her delicious mouth. "Sounds like you passed muster with the girls?"

She raises an eyebrow. Her face looks somber, and her gaze bypasses me, a distance in her eyes. "You weren't wrong about

Jess. She put me through a full interrogation. I felt like I was on *Dateline* or something."

"I'm sorry about that. But you clearly did well because she texted me her approval."

"Really? What'd she say?"

I shrug. "Do you want to read it?"

She nods.

Grabbing my phone and unlocking it, I hand it to her. As her eyes descend downward, she shakes her head, frowning. Definitely not the response I expected. What happened to her cute blushing? She looks down, her lips pressed firmly together. It feels like a Grand Canyon of distance sits between us, and I can't understand what's happening.

I lift my hand, ready to snag her under the chin and make her look me in the face. But she stops me dead in my tracks, asking flatly, "How was your day?"

A rumble of laughter fills my chest, and I hear Trix groan behind us, rustling dissatisfied in his crate. "Where would you like me to begin?"

Her eyes round, and her lovely lips part.

"Let's see. I taught Cole how to throw a frisbee. The kid doesn't have a half-bad arm. Then, my brothers showed up, and we headed next door to start working on your home repairs. I'm sorry to report that didn't last long, and we didn't get much done because...there was just a lot of other stuff we had to do..."

I trail off, still processing everything, and taking another gulp of the fruity, acidic, earthy blend. "Darlene from CPS showed up for a surprise visit. So, we had to tour the house to prove you and the kids are, indeed, staying with me. Which led to Rosie pointing out the fact you and I barely know each other. And, of course, that was a whole thing."

I don't tell her about Darlene's meltdown about Lily's and my age gap. Fortunately, Flynn and Logan were there to defend us and point out the significant age gaps in their own marriages. The whole conversation, while awkward and uncomfortable, needed to happen. Ever since the subject came up, I've been thinking differently about our fake marriage. For better or worse.

Lily covers her mouth, exhaling sharply.

"Don't worry, I told her the truth."

Lily swallows hard. "And what was that?"

"That I've had a thing for you since the first time I saw you..." My eyes try to capture hers, but she looks away.

"Okay," she mutters unconvinced.

What the fuck?

"Is there something the matter?" I question, my brows knotting.

"No," she says, taking another gulp of wine. But if there's something I've already learned, my wife is a terrible liar.

Chapter Twenty-Two

LILY

Turner studies my face, his eyes overflowing with warmth. But is it warmth for me or warmth for the business deal I'm helping him secure? I'm so angry that I can barely look the handsome cowboy in the face.

In his grumbly low voice, he continues, "So, we got through Darlene's visit. After that, Logan couldn't find his fucking work gloves, and I hate to say it, Strawberry, but I knew exactly what happened to them. I lit into Cole's ass because the kid has to understand stealing is a crime. Of course, that had him in tears, along with Poppy and Daisy. Rosie and Jack were oblivious to the whole scene. But I knew I was doing the right thing...until we ended up in your parents' garage looking for tools and stumbled across one of Trix's old beds."

I nod, remembering the extra bed in the garage.

Turner rubs his hand over his face. "I lifted the cushion and found Logan's gloves, countless unmatched pairs of my welding gloves, and some of my smaller tools. More or less everything I've ever accused Cole of stealing. So, yeah, you've got a fucking packrat for a dog."

142

"More like a klepto," I gasp. Shooting daggers towards the crate with my eyes, I scold, "What a bad puppy!"

"Needless to say, I spent about an hour apologizing to Cole and the other kids. After that, we went to Hollister to get cookies at Cricket's bakery. Thank goodness she bent the rules and kept Sweet Rush open late for us..."

"How nice of her..." I interject, trying to sound cheerful.

He nods, his baby blues continuing to dig into me as if he's looking into my soul. *Boy, this man can put on a good act.* "After Sweet Rush, we headed to the Merc to look for Pokemon cards. Cole didn't like what they had, so we got some cool vintage comic books instead. It's selfish, but I hope to spark the kid's love of them and maybe baseball cards. If I can do that, I've got a whole collection of both that'll keep him busy for a while."

My eyes fill with tears as he talks about Cole. Not only is Turner using me, but he's using my siblings, too. My heart breaks thinking about them getting hurt by this fake marriage. Haven't they already been through enough?

He side-eyes me hesitantly. "I'm not saying something wrong again. Am I?"

"No," I shake my head, swiping at my cheeks. "These are happy tears. That boy needs a father figure..." My words mean to cut him, fill him with guilt. *If he's able to feel real guilt.*

To my disgust, he nods, answering, "Honestly, I don't know how good I'd be at filling that role. But if it makes you happy, I'll give it a shot."

"Of course you will," I answer caustically, Roxanne's words swirling in my head.

His eyes narrow, and he looks puzzled. "The other children got all sorts of useless shit that you and I will be picking up for God only knows how long. But at least we avoided Legos. My bro, Wolfe, warned me they're real motherfuckers when you step on them in the middle of the night."

My hand goes to my mouth to suppress a chuckle. Asshole or not, he's right, even if he is exploiting me for his own gain. *But aren't I doing the same to him?* Everything about this situation is impossible. Completely impossible.

His face relaxes at my change of demeanor, and I feel guilty for how I've acted tonight. But I'm heartbroken, and I should have known better. Maybe the person I'm maddest at isn't Turner at all. It's me.

"After that, we had a generally quiet evening... Except for spilled grape juice on the front area rug, an overflowing toilet that flooded the upstairs guest bathroom, umm...some kind of dirty handprints on the wall... I've still got to send samples of the residue for forensic testing... You know, the usual." He goes from talking to laughing and shaking his head. "Honestly, woman, I have no fucking clue how you do it from day to day."

My heart drops at his last few sentences, and my stomach knots into a tight ball of guilt. I look away reflexively, tears filling my eyes again.

A warm, strong finger hooks me under the chin, raising my gaze until I stare into his impossibly blue eyes. "Strawberry, don't cry. I wasn't trying to make you sad. It was just a crazy day."

"But we've destroyed your life, Turner. Don't you see? You had such a lovely house before we showed up and now look at it. I can't let you do this any longer. We've ruined everything for you. It's unfair."

It's also unfair to let my siblings get any closer to him if he is using me for a business deal... I keep this thought to myself, still not entirely convinced by Roxy's words, but shaken to my core. After all, Turner knows exactly why I entered into this fake marriage, but he has yet to tell me why he did.

He clears his throat. "The only thing that would ruin my life is...not getting to know you better."

"That's a good one," I reply, no longer able to suppress the angry tremor in my voice. "How long did you practice in the mirror to look so convincing?"

Turner's brows furrow, and his eyes storm. "Is there something I did to make you angry? Because you've been cold all evening, and the way you're looking at me now and talking doesn't make any sense."

"I don't want to talk about it." I sigh, letting my head fall back to stare at the ceiling in frustration.

"Now, I'm getting pissed because I haven't done anything wrong, and I don't have any idea what's going on," he growls. "Maybe the wine's not hitting you right. You should go to bed...sleep it off. I'll take the guest—"

"I used to live in France. I know how to tolerate wine..."

"Well, what is it, then?" He whispers, his voice growing louder with frustration. "Because I'm confused as fuck between your flirtatious texts from earlier and how you're acting now. It's like you've done a one-eighty."

"We should go to bed," I reply quietly.

"Fine," he says through gritted teeth.

Chapter Twenty-Three

TURNER

As my heart sinks, we go through the motions of putting away the wine and food. This scenario is how my past relationships have usually ended, with anger and miscommunication. But only after several years together and certainly not in less than forty-eight hours. This has to be a new record for me. Hell, I can't even rightly call what's going on between Lily and me a relationship...even though we're technically married.

I should've known better. *I did know better.* I remind myself of all the reasons I could never make her happy. She wants Paris, not some backwater hick-town. She wants a professional artist, not a weekend hobby sculptor. She wants an educated guy, not one who dropped out of college to go into construction. Millionaire or not.

I follow her upstairs, still fuming. My mind swims with possible explanations for her behavior. Is she PMSing? Did my sisters say something to her? Is she regretting this morning, even though she clearly consented? I don't fucking know.

At the door of the guest bedroom, I grab the handle, glancing over my shoulder and nodding goodnight.

Puzzlement clouds her face as she stops, too.

Am I forgetting something?

I rack my brain for a moment as her eyes examine me expectantly. Finally, I say, "We handled the chickens, so you don't need to go out there with your headlamp and wrestle bobcats."

Her face flushes, and she shakes her head. She opens her mouth, but nothing comes out.

So, I add, "And I'm sorry about not making the kids do whatever chores they're supposed to. But you're going to have to make a list because they sure as hell aren't going to volunteer that information to me."

She gulps air, shaking her head for a second time.

I stare at her, clearing my throat as an awkward silence settles between us.

What am I forgetting?

She inhales deeply and then exhales, her cheeks burning and her voice cracking. "Why are you staying in the guest bedroom? If the kids see us—"

I frown, wishing she would make this easier on me. "Honey, you made it abundantly clear tonight that I'm not what you're looking for. After this morning..." I swallow hard. "I thought things would be different. But you can barely stand to have a glass of wine with me and talk, let alone share a bedroom."

"Under the circumstances, what do you expect?" she whispers, her voice straining angrily. I step back, shocked by the vitriol pouring off her in waves.

"You mean, the fake marriage? I get it. I'm trying to make this easier on both of us, but there's no reason to be mad about it..."

One look at her wine-colored face lets me know she's livid. "Why did you marry me?" she hisses. "I want an answer and not that lame excuse you keep making about wanting to right a past wrong."

My face stiffens, and I clench my jaw. Through gritted teeth, I say, "There's nothing lame about it. I was referring to my mother and the second chance my family never got." My voice breaks, and I feel like a loser. Thank God I didn't allow myself to open up any more to this girl. She's proven tonight that I can't trust her.

"What do you mean 'chance you never got?'" Her green eyes fixate on me.

I shake my head. "No, we're not going there. Trust is earned, not given."

"Those are rich words coming from your lips..."

My mouth hangs open as rage radiates from her. I finish, "You know what? I'm done. I'm going to bed."

I turn on my heel towards the guest bedroom, but she grabs my arm. As angry as she's made me, I have trouble denying her. Every part of me wants her so badly. My whole body hurts, even as she eviscerates me without hesitation. This is why I hate love. It hurts like hell.

"You know, you're not even asking me the right question," I point out, my voice rising with rage. "Who cares why we got married? We both did it for the wrong reasons. You should be asking me why I think it could work between us. And why we'll both regret it if we don't give this relationship a shot."

I clench my jaw tightly, feeling the muscles ripple. My eyes scrutinize her surprised expression. "Do you want to see why I think—no, I know—we're right for each other, Lily?"

Her eyes round, stealing my heart despite my best attempts to guard it, and she nods without hesitation.

I motion for her to follow, heading downstairs to the kitchen slider that takes us out back. I grab a handheld camping lantern on the way, trudging toward the workshop and feeling like I'm a million years old.

I listen for her occasional footfall to ensure she's still behind me. At the workshop door, I rustle with the lock, frustrated. I thought Lily and I understood each other on some level. But despite my confident words a moment ago, I doubt everything except my foolish, inescapable feelings for her.

Turning on the lights, the workshop illuminates. Along the walls are a handful of chairs and couches for when artist friends and patrons come to visit. And there's a bar next to the seating, where I can throw together some basic cocktails and play music, depending on the vibe I'm trying to set. Especially for fellow Burners.

Behind me, Lily gasps, looking up at the massive metal statues looming above us. Some are commissions for public art projects around the world. Others are personal outlets for my creative passions. Most are in pieces and waiting to be assembled on-site.

I have a massive whale sculpture of a mother and baby that I'm working on for a public square in Barcelona. Designed to go in front of the city's main aquarium.

A huge spiraling array of intricate flames, spirals, and stars that I made for Burning Man three years ago looms large, and another of a massive mother's torso, cradling a baby in her arms. That one is personal—for the mother who never got to love me the way she wanted to. And the mother I wish I had more time with...despite everything.

In the center of the room towers the sensual lines of a curvy, gorgeous goddess that I started three months ago as "Gaia." A couple of months in and lots of soul-searching later, I admitted the truth about the statue's inspiration, renaming her "Lily."

The redhead's eyes went straight to a scaled-down model of this statue the first time she entered my cabin, fingering it and falling in love with it. It made everything leading up to that moment feel predestined. It also made showing her my workshop an inevitable impossibility.

Because it means telling her how much I love her...

"You're the sculptor who makes these?" Her voice is so breathless I have to lean in to make out her words.

I nod firmly.

"They're stunning...breathtaking." Tears fill her eyes. "But I don't understand. Why didn't you tell me you were an artist sooner?"

"The time wasn't right," I reply.

"And why are you showing them to me now?"

"Because before you decide to leave me, which I can already feel you're starting to do, you have to know what you mean to me. How beautiful and sensual and perfect you are to me... While words may fail me, I've poured some of what I feel for you into her. I know what I do is nothing compared to you. I don't have an art school education, apart from a few college courses. I create most of my projects to commission for cash. But I am an artist, which is what you said you wanted...a pretty well known artist, although I'm not trying to brag or make myself sound better than I am."

I point at the sexy goddess above our heads. "I call her 'Lily' for obvious reasons. She's far from completed, but I've worked on her for the last three months. I forced my brothers to help me with her all day because being around you...fills me with a kind of creativity that buzzes through my whole body. I have to find a way to express it or go mad." I nod, grimacing hard as tears fill my eyes.

I should have known better. Women always go away. That's how it is.

"She's gorgeous." I hear sniffling behind me, and my heart sinks. The last thing I want to do is make this woman cry. And I don't want her pitying me because I'm a lovestruck fool.

Maybe I shouldn't have shown her the sculpture. But she

needs to know how stunning she is to me...and the emotions she inspires in me...no matter what happens.

I feel her tiny hand grab mine, shifting to lace our fingers together, and I warn, "Don't touch me, Lily, I can't fucking do this with you anymore."

She squeezes my hand. "But I thought you married me to clench the business deal with Broderick..."

"What the fuck? Who told you that?" I growl, wheeling around to face her. I quickly wipe the back of my free hand over my eyes, looking away. Shit, she doesn't need to see me crying and know what a fucking loser I am.

She steps forward, palming my cheek and forcing me to look at her. "Roxanne overheard you talking with Broderick at the restaurant the last time she served you two. She said you were trying to get his company after he retires, and he said you needed to be married. Then, seeing how you're related to the sheriff who has connections to CPS, she figured you had arranged the whole thing to get me to marry you."

I shake my head, marveling at the raven-haired waitress's imagination. A pang of guilt hits me as I admit, "I'd be lying if the thought of getting the deal with Broderick never crossed my mind. But was it any worse than you marrying me to save your siblings?"

Lily shakes her head, looking down.

"I'll call Broderick right now and turn down the deal if that makes you feel better. But honestly, I haven't even told him we got married. It's been the last thing on my mind because all I can think about is you and making you so happy you won't leave me."

Her face softens, but I have more to say.

"As for the rest of it? No, just no. I can't believe you'd ever think such a thing of me. We still have a lot to learn about each other, but I hope you know I'm a man of honor. And as for Christian, you should realize he'd never do something like that...especially so I could take advantage of a vulnerable woman."

The beautiful redhead slips her fingers away from mine, bringing both hands to her face. "I don't know what I think, Turner. I just know I fucking love you. It's irrational. It makes no sense, and I'm pretty damn sure you're going to break my heart. Or I'm somehow going to mess it up...like I just did."

"You love me?" I repeat quietly, letting the implausible words sink in.

Sobbing, she says, "See what I mean? Now I ruined everything even more by saying 'I love you' first. You may avoid relationships because you aren't a big fan of commitment. But I avoid them because I'm a wrecking ball. I mean, Miley Cyrus has nothing on me when it comes to destroying shit...because I always know how to—"

With a powerful stride, I cross the distance between us, pulling Lily into my arms and capturing her lips with mine. She tastes like the ocean, tears pouring down her face. I devour her unhesitatingly, kissing her the way I imagine a husband would, pouring all of my love and soul into her.

I would die for this woman. That's how much I love her, and I still don't fully understand why. But I can't ignore it any longer...

Pulling back, I palm her cheeks, staring into her stunning face. "You may have said it first, but I've been thinking it since the moment I laid eyes on you. I love you, Lily. I love you so fucking much it hurts. I can't think straight because of you, and there's nothing I wouldn't do to make you happy. Like sell-my-kidney happy if that's what it takes."

She looks shocked, and I nod in agreement, fully conscious of how crazy I sound.

"I know you think you want Paris and big cities and all that shit... I get it. I was twenty-one once, too. But I'm here to tell you, what you want is me...us. What we can become together. Paris is like any other city in the world. Planes fly there daily, and I've got the money to take us whenever we like. But this—" I grab her hand and place it over my heart so she can feel it beating. "This is all we need to be happy."

"Yes," she says, smiling and crying simultaneously. "You're all I want and need forever, Turner."

I wrap my arms around her, planting my mouth firmly over hers as I press her backward into the wall. God, her soft body feels good against mine. A growl escapes my lips as my mouth moves over her wine-flavored lips. I bring my hand to her cheek, savoring its softness before tipping her head to deepen my stroke.

Standing on her tiptoes, she snakes her arms around my neck, and I pull her off her feet, twirling her around. *I feel like I've won the fucking lottery.*

Chapter Twenty-Four

I set her back down, and the mood turns serious and desperate. I let my tongue linger over the line in her lush lower lip before sinking into her mouth for another taste. Returning the kiss fervently, she matches every passionate stroke of my tongue with her own until I'm crazed with need.

My hands drop to her hips again, those luscious, gorgeous hips that I can't stop dreaming about. I grind her firmly against my stiff rod, involuntarily moaning at how her soft flesh yields to me. I should have more restraint, but I'm burning alive—well past the reach of reason or logic.

I'm ready to drop to my knees right here, unbutton the front of her jeans, throw her leg over my shoulder, and dive into her pussy. After this morning, she's the only flavor I crave.

But Lily's got other plans. Her dainty fingers are already tugging at the button and zipper of my jeans. My head swims with want, and my heart feels like it's about to explode.

Her hand slides into the front of my boxer briefs before I can warn her. But it's too late.

Her eyes round, and her jaw drops.

I laugh knowingly.

"You seriously have a Prince Albert?"

A lopsided grin captures my face as I growl in low tones, "You're the one with your hand in my shorts. You tell me."

She massages into me, and I groan, closing my eyes and breathing hard. "Fuck, you're no angel, Strawberry."

"I don't get it. Is this a secret cowboy thing, and the joke's on all of us city girls?"

Her question makes me chuckle until she kneads into me again, replacing my laugh with a needy moan. Breathlessly, I say, "I'm the only cowboy you need to worry about, city girl. And to answer your question, it's a make-my-woman-feel-good kind of thing, which means it's all yours."

She wraps her dainty fingers around my cock, pumping it and making me mindless. Fuck, I'd sign over my worldly wealth if she asked me.

"You don't have a thing against piercings?" I tease, stepping closer to her and wrapping my hand possessively in her hair before claiming her mouth again like a ravenous wolf.

She pulls back, smiling wickedly and saying, "I think you already know the answer to that question."

"Yes, I do," I say, grabbing her breasts and rubbing my thumbs greedily over her nipple barbells. "I used to have my tongue pierced, too. But it wasn't a good look for a home-builder. I assure you, though, I know plenty of ways to make up for the missing barbell."

She whimpers.

Thank goodness I spent money on motion-controlled heat for this workshop last year because I don't want dropping temperatures interrupting us. I still grab the remote next to the couch, turning it up a few degrees. The last thing I want is the coolness of night to make her reluctant to slip out of her clothes.

Kissing her neck, I trace the line up to her earlobe before

flirtatiously nibbling it and then letting my tongue circle the shell of her ear. She exhales loudly. Leaning in, I whisper, "I hope you're not too tired after your girls' day out because this is gonna take all night."

Her eyes transform into molten desire at my words.

Frantically, I pull off her jean jacket and unzip the back of her dress, letting the fabric fall to her waist. I palm her ample tits, savoring their weight and softness before circling her pebbled and pierced nipples with my thumbs again.

"Have you ever been with a guy who has his dick pierced?" I ask.

Her cheeks flush as she shakes her head.

"Well, I've been told you're in for a treat. But before we get to the main course, I'm going to need a nice helping of dessert," I say, walking her backward towards the couch. "And a lesson in how these work," I say, flicking my thumb across her nipple. "So that I can bring you maximum pleasure."

"I'm clean and on the pill," she pants, anticipating where this is going.

"I'm clean, too," I reply. "And I've got plenty of condoms back at the house. But I think you'll like me better raw."

Her hand finds my steel-hard rod again, massaging it and running her thumb over the metal. Swallowing loudly, she says, "I want you raw."

"Fuck, woman, you're going to kill this old man if you keep talking to me that way and looking at me like that. I can take one or the other, but not both at the same time."

She laughs, looking dazed as I slide her dress over her luscious hips, memorizing every inch of her curvy body. The way her emerald lace bra hugs her ample breasts makes my mouth water. And her green panties have shifted to the side, giving me a peek at one half of her camel toe. *Shit and fuck, I need her now.*

I flick the clasp at the back of her bra, and it falls between us as my eyes hungrily devour her perfect ivory tits with their rosebud nipples pierced with steel. Greedily, I take her nipple in my mouth, swirling my tongue around her areola and flicking the barbell.

She gasps, melting into me as I suck and tease her, not stopping until she's breathless, and I move to the other side. Her fingers thread through my hair as a wild cry escapes her mouth.

My cock's about to explode, a realization that pulls me reluctantly from my exploration. I nudge her back onto the couch, kneeling in front of her. Grabbing her hips, I turn her so that her lovely pussy's in my face. I want with every ounce of my being to make our first time together so mind-blowing that she'll never leave me.

She looks stunned as she reclines back.

"What?" I ask.

"What happened to the boring old guy I thought I married?"

"That's the first assumption you made about me that we need to correct. I am a boring old guy with everyone...*except my woman.*"

"Corrected," she manages breathlessly.

"Now, it's time for me to demand some of that strawberry shortcake my mouth's been watering for." I place her legs over my shoulders, and she shudders in anticipation.

Realization flashes across her face. "Wait, is that why you call me 'Strawberry?'"

I raise my eyebrow, grinning. "Not the only reason, but it might be one of them. And just so you know, it's my favorite fucking dessert. Lie back and relax while I eat my fill."

"Fuck," she replies, her eyes dilating. "But you haven't even tasted me yet..."

"I'm about to rectify that," I pant. My eyes register the wet spot on the front of her green lacy panties, making me breathe harder. She's already dripping for me. Grabbing the lacy fabric, I pull it over her legs to the ground before getting an eyeful of her gorgeous, scarlet-hued landing strip.

She keeps it trimmed just the way I like it. And while I see ink on her chest, arms, thighs, and other places I long to explore, there's nothing on her breasts or pussy. Thank goodness because I'm a jealous man and couldn't stand the thought of a tattoo artist anywhere near my property.

I just hope she had a female pierce her nipples. But I push the thought from my mind. The past's the past. All I want to focus on now is making her scream my name.

My fingers and mouth go straight for her gorgeous pink pussy. I splay her arousal-shiny lips open with the pointer and middle fingers of my right hand, devouring her semi-aroused pearl.

Moaning deep in my throat, I relish her musky flavor as her hips strain towards my mouth. I run my tongue up and down her slit, greedily drinking every drop of her honey. Her back arches, and I fuck her silky channel with my tongue. She covers her mouth with one hand, trying not to scream. Her other hand grips one of the couch's accent pillows until it's a tight knot in her fingers.

I circle her clit with my tongue, teasing her pearl with my teeth and lips as I suck her in and out of my mouth, savoring the way her pink bud swells. She lets out a frantic exhale, and my tongue returns to her slit, licking her from her ass crack to her swollen nub until she sounds like she's hyperventilating. Then, I suck her pussy lips, teasing and nipping her—savoring the taste of her arousal.

Her delicious thick thighs spread wide, offering everything to me, and her hips curve towards my face as her hand comes to my head, gripping my hair and pushing me into her.

A delicious fork in the road greets me. Do I play with her

nipple barbells? Or do I sink into that delectable pussy of hers with my fingers?

As much as I want to know how her piercings work, I need to make her come again. What happened this morning already has me addicted to pleasing her. Each sharp exhale, each twist of her body, brings me closer to seeing that glorious moment repeated. I won't stop until I've stamped my claim on her body and soul. She'll beg for me and me alone.

The fingers of my left hand slide through her silky arousal. Her breath catches in her throat as she whispers, "Turner. Yes, please don't stop."

"Say it again," I command.

"Don't stop."

"With my name, Lily."

"Don't stop, husband."

My breath catches. "I love that word on your lips," I confess, my voice raw with emotion. I feel like the luckiest man on the planet. My finger melts knuckle deep into her, granting her wish. She lets out a hiss, clamping her hand over her mouth.

"We can take this as slow or as fast you like, wife," I tease, working my finger sensually in and out of her, feeling the velvety wet warmth of her pussy. I let my mind wander to how it'll feel wrapped around my thick cock.

She cries out, her hips arching into my hand. I feel her walls thickening, swelling, and gripping my finger tightly. *Fuck yes.* "You set the pace, woman, by telling me how much you want me."

She breathes shallowly as I deepen the stroke of my finger, dropping my mouth to her clit and circling it greedily, accompanied by wicked wet noises. Her pussy squeezes my finger erratically as I take her closer and closer to the edge.

"Turner, I want you so badly."

"Do you?" I tease, moving my finger to focus on the rough

spot near the front of her pussy that I know will make her scream. She squirms under the pressure of my merciless finger and mouth, but I won't let her go until she drenches my hand again.

"I need you inside me, Turner. I need your cock more than anything. I can't fucking take it anymore."

Her hands go to her pierced nipples, and I watch her flick and twist them, taking notes on what heightens her desire. Her face is flushed and needy, and her legs tremble as her core tightens.

"Beg me to make you come, Lily."

"Please, Turner. Please. I need you to make me—" She screams my name as her hips buck up towards my face, and she covers my hand in her cum. It's the loveliest sight I've ever seen. And the feel of her pussy tightening around my finger and sucking me in nearly undoes me. My cock jumps, ravenous for a piece of the action.

Chapter Twenty-Five

LILY

"**W**hat do you want from me?" Turner whispers, his eyes black with desire.

I bite my lower lip, saying. "First, I want you out of those clothes—completely. And then I want to test drive that fancy gadget you showed me earlier."

"Yes, ma'am," he says, standing up and making quick work of granting my wish. I suck in a startled breath as my eyes rove over his gorgeous, muscled physique. He's a masterpiece, from his broad shoulders to his well-defined abs and tapered waist.

A teasing strip of hair at the bottom of his abdomen leads my eyes to his thick, erect cock and the round silver where his barbell runs through the head of his shaft. Leaning forward, I take him in my mouth, letting my tongue flick and tease his piercing.

He lets out a contented sigh. "Fuck, yeah, baby."

Savoring the smoothness of his rod, I let my tongue and lips dance over him, loving the way every movement draws him closer to blissful abandon. Wrapping my hands around the backs of his thighs, I relax my throat, ready to take him deeper.

But he stops me, withdrawing slowly from my mouth.

His eyes close in concentration, and he wraps his hand around the base of his dick, saying, "I need your pussy, Strawberry."

He sits on the couch beside me, motioning for me to straddle him. My pussy's still so swollen from earlier that every movement nearly sets me off again as I reposition myself.

His hand comes up to palm my cheek, and his eyes well as I slowly slide down over his rigid rod. He lets out a moan of pleasure, and I watch through a blur of tears as his face transforms into ecstasy.

"Damn, woman," he whispers, grabbing my waist with both hands and thrusting into me as I scream. "It's better than I ever imagined." His eyes snap open, and he says with a seductive grin, "And just for the record, I've done a lot of imagining. Fuck, Strawberry. You're all I want in this world."

I clamp my hand over my mouth, trying to capture the scream that grips me at the feel of his rod and piercing, stimulating my G-spot. He's almost too big, but my pussy sucks him in greedily. I arch back, breathing fast as his lips find my nipples, and he twists and teases me into oblivion.

I writhe on top of him, climaxing hard as pleasure rocks my core, and I tremble and spasm, riding waves of ecstasy. He follows behind, releasing into me with a roar. Pulsing heat into me, he wraps himself tightly around my waist, resting his head on my soft breasts.

Our breathing slows as he holds me tightly, enveloping me in love and security.

"Your pussy is perfect. Why have you kept it from me for so long?"

I laugh, lazily stroking his cheeks and relishing in the feel of his five o'clock shadow under my palms. My hands descend to his rock-hard shoulders and chest, roving over every angular inch of him. "Are you being serious right now? We despised each other less than forty-eight hours ago."

He laughs deep in his throat, kissing me tenderly. "Which means I've got plenty of wasted time to make up for... I hope you realize what you've gotten yourself into. I'm a greedy lover, Lily," Turner warns darkly. "Hell, I'm already strategizing seven ways from Sunday to make you scream my name and lose your mind again."

"I like the sound of that," I purr. "Tell me about those seven ways from Sunday," I intone seductively.

He slides his hands down over my naked ass, squeezing my hips. "Let's see," he says, looking up at the ceiling for a moment and then back at me. "Well, for starters, I want my cock pressed between your delicious tits, and I want it throat-deep in that beautiful mouth of yours. I'd give your tight, sweet ass a try, too."

"Not with that thing," I protest. "You're huge!"

He smiles seductively, "There are countless ways I can please you, Strawberry."

My cheeks burn, and he kisses them, exclaiming, "This will never get old... See, you're already distracting me... What were we talking about?"

"Seven ways from Sunday?"

"Oh, yeah," he growls. "I definitely need you bent over this couch while I eat you out from behind before pounding you mindless. And the shower...shit, I have way too many ideas for the shower. I can't wait to wake up next to you in bed for a sleepy round of morning sex... But more than anything, I want you seated on my face with those thick thighs of yours squeezing my cheeks."

"But what if I suffocate you?"

"Suffocate me?" he says incredulously. "I can't think of a better way to exit this planet."

"Are you serious right now?"

"Hell, yeah. I'll sign a damn waiver if it makes you feel better. Know this, though, Strawberry, your pussy's mine for keeps. And I'm going to enjoy the hell out of it every chance I get and from every angle my mind can dream up." He nods towards the sculptures towering over us. "And as you can see, I've got a pretty intricate imagination."

"You know, I'm taking mental notes, and I'm going to hold you to every single one of these promises you're making—"

"I haven't scared you yet?" he asks, disbelief etched on his face.

I shake my head, chuckling softly. "You're right about me keeping my pussy away from you for too long, though. With a game plan like that, we could've used a head start."

"No, this is perfect," he replies, a raw edge coloring his voice.

I love him so much, I can't help myself. I kiss and caress his face and neck, savoring every moment of discovery, the feel of his hard flesh beneath my lips, and the masculine taste of him. I want him to feel how desperately and madly I love him in every inch of his being.

He says quietly, "I fantasized about fucking you often. But I never thought about how tender you'd be with me. Or how you'd make me feel like I mean something to you."

His words surprise me, and my mouth falls open as I say, "You mean everything to me, Turner. There's not a part of you I don't love. I want it all, the good and the bad, the ugly and the beautiful—"

He cups my cheeks, staring intensely into my eyes, "For richer, for poorer, in sickness and in health..."

"To love and to cherish until death do us part," I finish running my hands through his thick brown hair and feathering my lips over his face. Admiring every gorgeous inch of him as the gravity of the moment sets in.

Squeezing me possessively, he declares, "I don't like that ending. We're going to rewrite it. Love is stronger than death... Never forget that, Strawberry."

Epilogue

TURNER

ONE MONTH LATER

After dropping the kids off at Wolfe and Izzie's for a play date with their two kids, Lily and I drive to the center of Rough & Ready Ranch for an afternoon horseback ride.

It's the kind of mid-March day that convinces you Jack Frost has packed his bags and headed north for the spring. But I know better. Next week, we could get hit with a blizzard that dumps ten feet of snow. Mother Nature's finicky and unpredictable at sixty-five hundred feet.

"I don't know if I'll be any good at this," Lily says for the twentieth time. But excitement is written all over her face.

"You've got nothing to worry about," I croon, squeezing her hand as it rests on my thigh. "I told Sonny to tack up Marshmallow for you. She's the sweetest mare in the stable."

Lily's face beams, even though I still read hesitation in her eyes.

"You know I won't let anything happen to you, woman. You're my world now."

"I know," she says, looking up at me with her big green doe eyes, overflowing with trust and love.

Inside the stables, we pass Sonny, the crimson-haired high schooler who mucks stalls. I nod and grumble, "Hello."

But Lily's more exuberant with her greeting, "We could be brother and sister!"

The teen laughs bashfully, and Lily looks confused by his awkwardness. She still doesn't realize how drop-dead gorgeous she is. Or that men of every age and station have to roll their tongues back in their mouths after seeing her.

I wrap my arms around her, kissing her fervently. The woman in my arms owns every inch of my heart and soul, but I worry about being enough for her. About whether Rough & Ready can hold her despite the beck and call of Paris...

Sonny's got both horses ready to go. We head out into the yard, where I give her a run-through of the basics. Then, she practices proper mounting and posture. Once she's seated in the saddle for the first time, her face lights up with newfound confidence.

Marshmallow's as mellow as it gets. The fat old white mare nuzzles my neck and chest, nibbling on the front pockets of my Carhartt. I give her liberal pats while Lily gets accustomed to the feel of everything.

Next, we go over communicating with the horse through her legs and seat. Like all newbies, she wants to do everything with her hands. I remember my foster dad Wyatt patiently teaching me these same things many years ago when I was only a bit older than Poppy.

As if reading my mind, she exclaims, "We've got to bring the kids out to do this."

"We should," I say, pleased as punch by the exhilaration written all over her face.

Once she consistently holds the reins close or at the wither, I jump on Bugsy. A sporty little buckskin, he's my go-to for steer roping and always raring to go. But today, we're taking it easy. After a few minutes, he settles into Marshmallow's leisurely pace.

I ride a little behind Lily, making sure she's okay. "How are you feeling, Strawberry?"

Glancing over her shoulder, she says, "This is freaking amazing! I'm starting to see why you cowboys spend so much time in the saddle."

I chuckle. "We'll see what you think two hours from now."

Her mouth falls open. "How long are we riding for?"

"One hour in and one hour back with a nice long break in between. You think you're up for that?" Guilt pricks me. I've been thinking so much about why I want to ride where we're headed. I haven't considered her needs. Maybe the trip will push her too far, too soon.

A radiant smile captures her face. "I don't think it's nearly long enough."

Squeezing Bugsy with my legs, I cue him forward, bringing me to Lily's side. Grabbing her hand, I say, "We'll see what your ass has to say about it later, city girl. That said, I can't help but think you look like you were made for this. Hell, I think you're the hottest fucking cowgirl I've ever seen."

"Well, I've had plenty of practice..."

I ask, "How do you mean?"

"Riding a cowboy." Her cheeks darken.

"You have a point," I clear my throat, one month's worth of delicious memories washing over me. My heart pounds, and I grin from ear to ear. "If you can handle me and still walk straight, this'll be nothing for you."

"I love you."

The words surprise me, considering the current topic of conversation. "Where did that come from, Strawberry?"

"Everything about this moment. This place. Being here

with you. I've never seen beauty like this before...not even in my dreams." Her head bobbles around, and she inhales deeply, as if she's trying to gobble up every inch of the ranch's unfolding scenery with all five senses.

Her words fill my heart to bursting, buttressing my hope. "I love you, too. But this is nothing compared to where I'm taking you. If you start feeling tired, let me know. We can take a break anytime you like."

It's easy to take this place for granted sometimes, especially living here day in and day out. But as we continue riding, she lets me see it through fresh eyes. The distant snow-dusted Sierra Nevada tower, jagged and untamed.

Lily's breath catches in her throat as forested elevations give way to expansive meadows colored by the first wildflowers of the unfolding season. A creek babbles to our right.

"Are you staying warm enough?"

She nods as we finally enter the spot I've wanted to bring her ever since she asked me what I love about this place. Lily covers her mouth with her hand, gazing without speaking at the idyllic meadow that stretches on one side to towering old-growth forest and on the other to looming mountains. In the distance, I spy three does, silently gaining Lily's attention and pointing. We watch, barely breathing, until they catch our scents and sprint away.

I help Lily bring Marshmallow to a halt in the center of the meadow. The creek we followed here snakes through the middle, punctuated by a large Aspen grove. The trees' white-and-black papery bark stands in stark contrast to the promise of green leaf buds.

And beyond that are massive cedar trees, straining towards the sky. Beneath their bows in the shade of the forest's floor, the creek babbles, curling peacefully between impossibly thick reddish tree trunks. A fire pit in the natural shelter invites us to stay.

I rub my hand over my heart, feeling my pulse pounding. "What do you think?" My voice sounds a little breathless, and I don't know why.

"It's...beautiful, stunning. In my wildest dreams, I didn't know a place like this existed."

Taking a deep breath and feeling strangely vulnerable, I say, "I hope this answers your question about why I make Rough & Ready my home?"

Tears pour down her cheeks, and a bittersweet smile captures her lips. Wiping her hands over her face, she says, "And now I know why this place beguiled my parents, too..." I can tell she wants to say more, but her breathing comes faster now as if she's trying to suppress a sob.

"Do you think you could be happy here with me?" I ask in low tones.

Silence settles as she looks around, sweeping her head from side to side. Straining to take it all in at once.

She grabs my hand, gazing at me. "It speaks to my soul in ways I can't describe. As if the land is living and breathing."

I nod, relieved. She gets it. She gets me.

Lily continues, "I know it's only been a month. But I can't imagine being anywhere you're not. Ever. What in the world have you done to me?"

I grin. "You know, I could ask you the same thing, Strawberry. It seems like my entire happiness has somehow come to rest on making you happy. If that makes sense at all."

"It does, and I feel the same way," she confesses. More tears splash her cheeks, infused with love from her adoring gaze. I don't know what I did to deserve this girl. But I'll spend the rest of my life earning the privilege of having her all to myself.

"This is where I plan on marrying you properly, Lily. If you'll have me?"

"Of course I will," she replies, laughing. Her eyes sparkle

with joy. "Now, how do you get me off this thing so I can kiss my what? Husband? Fiancé?"

"Man. I'm your man forever, Lily. You can always count on me, and I'll never disappoint you if God gives me any say in the matter."

I hop off Bugsy and help Lily down, kissing her until she's breathless and wordless. Then, I begrudgingly release her to explore the cedar grove while I use a breakaway tie to secure the horses with enough slack to reach the creek for water and their food.

Pulling out the blankets and lunch I packed for our expedition, I set up a spot inside the secluded cedar grove to recline. My woman reaches straight past the food for me, and we make love in the cool of the trees, delighting in the two bodies and lives we're weaving into one.

Afterward, my fingers and lips wander slowly over her beautiful tattoos. Savoring the feel of her skin and ink and the tremendous beauty of her inner artist's soul. I know it sounds cheesy, but her soul truly feels like my other half.

As the late afternoon sunlight gives way to twilight, I build a fire in the pit. We snuggle and talk, making love with our hands and diving into the meal that I intended hours ago for lunch. I brought wine, and we drink it from the bottle. I think back to the first time we drank this stuff together and the pain and bliss that smacked into me that night.

I clear my throat. "I've made you wear my mother's silly old ring long enough. We'll go shopping this next week in Sacramento or San Francisco, and I'll get you anything you want. Your heart's desire."

She looks down at the humble little band and its small diamond, trying so hard to make up for its size with shine. "No, I like this ring, and I want to keep it. If you're okay with that?"

Her words catch me so off guard that silence overtakes us.

"Okay with that?" Emotion knots in my throat. "Of course, I'm okay with that. I gave it to you. But we do need to get you a proper wedding band."

"And we can get a matching one for you...unless you want to keep wearing my dad's. I mean, it's not my dad's anymore. It's yours."

I nod. "It's settled then."

"Tell me about your mother." Despite the imperative of her words, her voice is so soft I have to lean closer to hear her.

"My mother's name was Leah. She had long brown hair that she kept piled on top of her head or in braids. Everything about her, from how she dressed to how she talked, exuded creativity. She was an idealistic artist and poet who spent more time in her head than in reality. Too young to be a mama and too hippie-dippy to function in life... But these deficits didn't make me love her any less. She just couldn't get herself pulled together. So, I cared for her, along with my two younger siblings."

Lily snuggles into me.

"The day CPS took us from her, I'll never forget." I pause, working hard to steel my voice. "I thought it was all my fault. And it tore me apart that I couldn't protect or shield her. Leah was too good for this world...and an amalgam of its faults. Between the drugs, alcohol, poverty, and bad men, CPS had to intervene. I understand that. But she died of a drug overdose not too long after. I always felt it had something to do with losing us. Like she just gave up..."

"I'm sorry," Lily whispers, feathering her lips over my neck and shoulders and holding me tightly.

"That was the past I had to correct with you and your siblings. Not that I thought you'd end up the same way. You're so much stronger and more resilient than my mom. But I couldn't stand to watch the world, and all of its responsibilities, crush another beautiful soul...the most beautiful soul I've ever known."

Her mouth finds mine, lifting the pain of those memories from me and lightening my heart. After loving and enjoying each other's bodies some more, Lily gasps, "It's getting dark. We won't be able to go back now."

"Why not?" I ask, amused.

"It's almost too dark to see."

I chuckle. "Horses can see just as well in twilight as daylight. We may not know where we're going, but I assure you they will. That said, it's getting chilly out here. So, we should think about dressing and packing back up. But first..."

I shuffle through the saddlebag next to me, pulling out the prenup. "Do you remember this?" Handing it to Lily, memories flood me of the Ophir City Courthouse parking lot and the swirl of strange feelings accompanying our fake marriage.

"I do," she says quietly.

Before she can react, I throw the papers into the flames of the fire, and Lily gasps. I say, "In case you doubted the sincerity of my devotion..."

She covers her mouth, shock written all over her face. Palming my chest, she says, "I hope you understand that I'd love you if we were both homeless and had to keep a cardboard box together by the side of the road. You didn't need to burn the prenup to prove your feelings to me."

"No, I had to burn it because now you're flesh of my flesh, blood of my blood. Everything I have is yours."

Nuzzling into my neck and running her hand down my chest, she replies, "All I want is you. Not what you have or hope to gain in the future. I want you—your beautiful heart and unmatched soul—all of you for the rest of my life."

* * *

Want more from Lily and Turner as they build a life and family together in Rough & Ready Country?

Read the bonus scene at https://www.engrideaves.com/freebies/.

* * *

I can't remember a time before Roxanne...or secretly loving her. But Milton, her older brother, is my lifelong best friend and Army National Guard buddy, which makes the curvy waitress off-limits.

But fate doesn't seem to get this. Everywhere I turn, the Native beauty's waiting for me, far more irresistible than she realizes. Of course, I've got plenty of excuses for keeping her at arm's length. I don't date rez girls. I don't date little sisters. And I don't cross the line between friends and lovers...

Until an unexpected night provides glimmers into a forbidden world of possibilities. Can I keep the gorgeous girl who haunts my dreams? Or will crossing the line mean losing everything? Devour the next steamy installment in the Rough & Ready Country series, *Love at First Night*: https://www.engrideaves.com/love-at-first-night/.

Also by Engrid Eaves

ROUGH & READY COUNTRY

Love at First Blizzard - He's a reclusive mountain man who runs a husky rescue, but his world gets turned upside down by the curvy classical musician he saves from a freak March blizzard.

Love at First Campfire - She's a headstrong, curvy true crime reporter who's never needed anybody until a handsome search and rescue unit lead risks everything to save her.

Love at First Rescue - He's a small-town sheriff who plays by the rules until his sexy dispatcher changes up the game, initiating a rescue that sets long-time passions ablaze.

Love at Second Chance - She's the new home health nurse in Rough & Ready Country, but miles of history with the grumpy ranch foreman are in danger of reigniting, despite her best intentions.

Love at First Baby - He's a wildland firefighter who refuses to settle down for anyone until the curvy hometown sweetheart and an unexpected baby make him reconsider what and who he's living for.

Love and Forgiveness - She's a museum director trying to move on until her estranged husband's security company wins her facility's contract, resurrecting long-buried passions.

Love at First Relationship - Everything about my paralegal, Jasmine, is off-limits as my much younger, inexperienced employee. But a fake relationship proposal quickly blossoms into much more.

Love at First House - A marriage of convenience is the only way to help my neighbor keep her family together. I tell myself it's a practical arrangement, but my heart has other plans.

Love at First Night - He's a helicopter pilot crushing on his best friend's little sister, Roxy. An unexpected night gives them a glimmer into a world of possibilities, but will love or heartbreak prevail?

HUNTER'S GUILD: ELITE BOUNTY SERVICES

Possessed by the Bounty Hunter - A six-figure bounty draws me back to my ex-fiancée and her mafia-linked Creole family. Soon, a centuries-old curse blurs the line between hunter and hunted.

About the Author

Engrid Eaves publishes short, sweet, and steamy romances featuring gruff alpha male protectors and the headstrong, curvy girls they fall head over heels for.

Her heroes may have painful pasts, but they always find forever with their soulmates. Sexy, satisfying, heartfelt happily ever afters guaranteed!

If you'd like to stay in touch or get your next delicious mountain man, curvy girl romance fix (and who doesn't?), sign up for her newsletter: www.engrideaves.com.

goodreads.com/engrideaves

bookbub.com/profile/engrid-eaves

instagram.com/engrid_eaves

tiktok.com/@authorengrideaves

facebook.com/EngridEavesAuthor